After Dad

Margaret Pitz

riverrun

For all their support and
encouragement along the way:

Caroline, Fran, Gillie
Hiag, Joyce, Justine, Nick

ONE

Shadowlands was on. In this version C S Lewis was played by Anthony Hopkins and Debra Winger was Joy Gresham. Her father had an old tape where Joss Ackland and Clare Bloom played the roles and she thought, on balance, she preferred them. Anthony Hopkins was too well-known to her now in other contexts; she couldn't quite believe in him as Lewis. He wasn't the right comfortable shape somehow.

But she watched it anyway, and then borrowed the tape of the other version and played it again. And bits of it again. Actually she lost count of how many times she watched it but she knew it was helping. As she eventually drifted off to sleep, replaying some of the scenes in her mind, she thought it very likely that Will, had he lived, could have been quite like Joss Ackland's portrayal of C S Lewis. Had he been allowed to, he might very well have grown old looking like him, too. Perhaps not quite so plump, but definitely comfortable and teddy bear-like. She wondered if either of them – Ackland or Lewis; obviously Will was not – was still alive. She would look them up tomorrow, right after she'd reviewed her latest writings on Will and Ariel Durant.

'May I buy some books?'

Howard was doing the breakfast washing up, in her experience a good time to approach him without getting too deeply involved.

'Course you can – what are you buying? I shouldn't think there are any books left about that American man you're so keen on.'

'Oh nothing important really, I thought I'd like to read things by C S Lewis. You know, the man in Shadowlands.'

'The Narnia Chronicles? Aren't you a bit old for them?'

'Maybe, but he wrote other things too. He wrote about finding her and then about losing her. That's what I'm really interested in.'

She sensed his discomfort at her raising, however obliquely, the topic of Will and his death, but she knew she'd got the OK she wanted and that her father had already lost interest in the books, so she muttered her thanks and left the kitchen. He wouldn't have been able to tell, but inside she was bubbling with an excitement she hadn't felt for several months at the prospect of reading what Lewis had written about his joy and his sorrow. She loved his titles – Surprised by Joy and A Grief Observed – and had kept saying them to herself over and over since she'd learned about them.

TWO

Saturday

Dear Will,

I have to say – again! – this way of journaling is so much better for me than just straight writing in a notebook. This way I can imagine you reading what I write, smiling or frowning and responding, and I can often know what you'd say and when you'd smile. Or frown.

Did you know about C S Lewis? I'm sure you would have, though I don't think you ever mentioned him and I don't remember ever seeing any of his works on your (our!) bookshelves. And of course I haven't been allowed to have anything from the house so I can't find out now if there were any. I'm currently mad about him and have just bought the two books he wrote that I thought were about his relationship with Joy Gresham: Surprised by Joy (which is a quote from Wordsworth, I think, and goes on: Impatient as the wind). As it turns out, it's actually about his conversion to Christianity, his acceptance of God, really, but I like the idea that he was 'surprised' by his love for Joy Gresham (or Davidman, sometimes called). After she died he wrote A Grief Observed and I'm finding that even more relevant to how I feel about losing you. (Oh don't you hate it when people say they 'lost' someone? You didn't lose him, he died!) Anyway, you know what I mean. (And it's easy to talk about somebody else's bereavement as dying, but not my own. I suppose that means I still haven't really accepted it. Well, that's what all the counsellors would say. Which of course is why I don't go and see any of them any more.)

Anyway, back to Dr Lewis. His mother died when he was only nine and he didn't get on with his father until he (his father) was dying. You'd love what he writes about grief. I know I do.

3

He says your body feelings in grief are the same as the feelings you get when you are afraid. Butterflies in your stomach, can't eat, can't sleep, can't concentrate, keep going hot and cold, feelings of impending doom. Somehow it helps to think of these feelings (that DO NOT get any better, despite what all the well-meaning people keep telling me) as fear.

So, fear of what? I hear you asking. Going through life without you, that's what.

I think Will and Ariel would have loved him (Dr Lewis). I can just imagine them being best friends. There would be the American connection from Joy Gresham and the philosophy and scholarly connection because that's what they both are. Except he was quite religious, that might have been a problem. Oh Will, how lovely it would be to be reading them with you and discussing it really with you, though of course if you were here I'd probably not have any reason to read it. Strange thought, and one I think both Will and Clive (his middle name is Staples, by the way, and his friends all called him Jack anyway) would relish discussing together. I don't think it would have mattered to Will and Ariel that he was an ardent (should that be fervent?) Christian. They might even have learned from him.

This is the sort of thing I'm supposed to be doing in my so-called home schooling, but I don't want to share these thoughts and feelings with anybody else but you. To keep the tutor happy I'll focus on the Wordsworth quote angle, and maybe ask about the difference between ardent and fervent. He's relatively easy to satisfy, actually and often seems quite astonished by my apparently unusually large vocabulary (thanks to you, by the way, for that). So as long as I say I'm reading or writing something, he's fine. I can't say I actually learn anything much from him though (except perhaps maths and some poetry). I often get the feeling that he doesn't know what I'm talking about. He certainly doesn't know about the Story of Civilization. Which is fine with me. He's not right for discussing W&A with.

To be fair to him, though, he is teaching me more maths and I find I quite enjoy solving the numbers problems he sets me. Sort of like Killer Sudoku only not really.

Good night Sweet Will. I can't say 'sleep well' like we used to say to each other, because according to some people you have 'fallen asleep'.

I miss you so utterly.

•

The home schooling – and indeed the tutor – had been a great disappointment to her. She had hoped her tutor would be a man, preferably a fatherly type, but even though Paul was old enough to be just about anybody's great-grandfather, he was about as far removed from what she had yearned for as he could be and still be a human being. He came to the house every Monday and they had a telephone session every Friday. On the intervening days she was supposed to be doing schoolwork as agreed between them. And usually she did.

On the plus side, he'd lately been suggesting that apart from maths, she might be ready to go on to the local college where she could feel more challenged and interested. She had been looking at various options and had now signed up for a philosophy and logic course that would begin in September. She already knew it wouldn't be covering the Durants' work, of course, but even so she was keen to learn about other thinkers over the ages and to see what Will had meant when he'd said they hadn't approached the subject in a way that made it accessible to 'Joe Ordinary'. And after reading the two books by C S Lewis, she wondered what courses she might take that would expose her to more of his thinking. She'd asked Paul, who had suggested – 'but not this term; you're not ready yet' – theology and religious studies, or medieval literature. She was pretty sure Will would not like her to take the former, and the college didn't offer the latter, so she did not pursue it.

Was she drifting away from their original purpose, hers and Will's? The thought made her uncomfortable; she knew Will would want her to go on, to write the next chapter in their continuation of the Durants' Story of Civilization. But without Will there to guide her, she didn't know how she could do that. Ever since he'd been killed and her life had turned upside down and inside out, she had thought and thought about the work they had done together since he had bestowed the Ariel mantle on her, on her (new and second) eleventh birthday, and she had occasionally written a sentence or two in an attempt to elaborate. But in her heart of hearts she knew it was drivel and did nothing to advance the project.

At first the activity had helped her feel closer to the absent Will. Now she felt she was letting him down and couldn't always see his smiling face in her mind's eye. On the rare occasions in their time together when he had been displeased with her, his face had taken on a cold and unpleasant look. She had dreaded that look and was now desperately afraid that this was the image she would have of him if she carried on as she was: not doing the work, or not doing it well enough.

'What would Jack Lewis say about it?' she wondered aloud to herself, and immediately felt such a wave of shame at her disloyalty to Will and the Durants that she had to stop what she was doing and sit down.

●

'Welcome, what's your name?'

She'd had to sign up as Jessica Pike of course, but had been hoping to become Ariel Dee again, at least to her classmates. Even so, the question threw her off balance. She took a deep breath: start as you mean to go on, she thought, and said 'You've probably got me down as Jessica Pike, but actually I go by Ariel, Ariel Dee,' and looked at the instructor as confidently as she could manage, lips set in a straight line and head held steady, she hoped.

He put a tick by Pike, Jessica, in his register, smiled and said, 'Okay Ariel. Find a seat and get ready to hone your thinking.'

She scanned the room quickly then tucked herself into an empty space next to a dark-haired girl who was drawing flowers round the edges of her open notebook. The girl looked up and half smiled, 'Pat,' she said. So 'Ariel,' Ariel responded, and half smiled back. She could see that Pat had written inside the floral decoration:

Pat loves Glyn

her welsh rare bit

'A composer whose name I've forgotten – it doesn't matter in this instance anyway – said "he who likes not fine music is an ass". Someone else – I think it might have been Shakespeare, but again, it doesn't matter; these are red herrings, something we'll also talk about today – anyway, whoever it was said "the law is an ass". Therefore, I put it to you that we can deduce from those two statements that the law doesn't like fine music. True or false? Write down which, please, and say why.'

Ariel was enchanted. Oh she wasn't taken in by the question for a moment, but this was the kind of conversation and discussion she'd so often had with Will and something she had deeply missed. She glanced over at Pat and was slightly shocked to see she had written 'True' and was now chewing the end of her pen as she apparently pondered what to say in the way of an explanation. The girl looked at her.

'It's a trick question,' she whispered, 'it won't matter whether you put true or false.'

Ariel hoped she was wrong and wrote 'false', followed by what she hoped would please the instructor – and also Will, if he'd been able to see it – which was actually much more important. She'd explain to Pat later.

So, later, 'What did you mean, "it's a trick question"?' She and Pat were sitting on the grass outside the cafeteria, having drifted there together by silent but apparently mutual consent.

'Well it was really. The answer was so obvious that I thought it HAD to be designed to catch us out. That's how it is in the sixth form anyway – perhaps college lecturers will treat us a bit more like grown-ups. Hope so, anyway.' Pat rolled onto her back and gazed up at the sky. 'He's not unattractive though, is he? I wonder if he's married. How old do you think he is?'

Not knowing which of the three questions to answer, Ariel said 'I don't know,' which in fact covered all three. But she was intrigued and anxious not to give Pat the impression that she wasn't interested in the conversation. 'How old do you think he is?'

'Too old for me, I'm quite sure. Even though I've had loads of experience. In any case, I've got a boy friend. Sort of. You?'

'Not really. No, actually. And not really much experience,' she took a deep breath, 'though I've kissed an older man.'

'Yeah?'

Ariel heard the question mark, but lost her nerve and changed the subject back to Pat. 'How do you "sort of" have a boyfriend?'

'He's in prison at the moment, so technically I'm free to play around I suppose. If I wanted to, but I don't think I do. He'll be out in about three weeks anyway, which would be just about enough time for me to fall madly in love with Teach and then have to dump him. Or somehow manage two men. That might be quite interesting actually.'

Instinctively Ariel knew that 'kissing an older man' would never measure up in Pat's eyes, so she was glad she hadn't elaborated. Besides, she couldn't decide – if she ever told anyone about Will – whether she would position him as her dad or talk about him as her soon-to-be-lover-and-husband. Her own preference would be for the dad role, but something told her that Pat would find her a lot more interesting if she could think of Ariel as an about-to-be child bride. Her years of experience at sussing out the situation before committing to anything in particular would help her bide her time, and for the moment at least, it didn't seem necessary to contribute much to the conversation. Pat was only too happy to carry the burden, undoubtedly sensing that she had an eager enough listener in Ariel.

'My bloke's three years older than me, actually, which I quite like. How old is your older man?'

'Oh, he was over thirty, but really he was more my dad than a boyfriend.' Ariel made the sudden decision to stick with the truth as far as she could.

'So when you say "kissed him", do you mean that sort of kissing, or just a daughterly peck on the cheek?'

'No, a proper kiss, full on the lips.'

'Ooh, very Freudian! Do you still fancy him?' Pat sat up and looked admiringly at Ariel.

'Uhm…' she felt scared; this conversation was going too far, too fast and she didn't know how to manage it without being downright rude to Pat. She hadn't minded being rude to the counsellors and social workers, but amazingly Pat was already too important. Ariel wanted her friendship. 'Actually, he's dead. I can't talk about it. Not at the moment anyway.' She swallowed hard and mentally crossed her fingers that Pat would leave it – and her – alone.

Pat flopped back down onto the grass. 'Oh my god! That's awful. I've never known anybody who died. Sorry Ariel, I'll shut up now.' She sat up again and, leaning against the tree, kicked off her sandals and studied her shimmering yellow painted toenails.

Ariel tried to smile and tell Pat it was okay, but all she could manage was a grimace and shrug. They sat in silence for a few minutes, then Pat got to her feet.

'Have you any idea what you'll write for the homework assignment? I hardly even know what "conundrum" means, never mind giving him an example.'

'Not yet,' Ariel felt that was the right answer for Pat, although as soon as she'd heard the task her head had been filled with memories of Will testing her powers of logic and deduction, so her only hesitation was knowing which of the many examples she should offer. 'I'm liking the class though, are you?'

'Oh yes. The lecturer's easy on the eye and I've met you. What's not to like? See you on Tuesday, bye.' And she was gone.

THREE

Saturday

Dear Will,

It seems ages since I wrote to you. And I suppose that's because it IS ages. I've been busy reviewing my puerile writings about Will and Ariel D, I've been birding a bit (prompted by seeing a female bullfinch at the bus stop of all places) and I've started the philosophy and logic class at the local college. Nothing new to say about W&A – or about the birding either – so I'll tell you how much I'm enjoying the P&L course. Not least because I sit next to a girl called Pat whom I like a lot and who seems to like me. More about her in a minute.

So far the course is more about what the lecturer calls 'honing our powers of deductive reasoning' than about other philosophers. He wants to improve our logic, he says. Some of his challenges are ridiculously easy, for example: 'Hands up if you can't hear me: a sensible thing to say or not?' Nobody got that wrong of course, so he said he could see we are an above-average set, which makes me wonder what his previous groups have been like! Pat said he undoubtedly says that to every class to make them feel so good they'll do well for him by trying harder. She's probably right, she's very wise about things like that. In fact, about a lot of things.

The assignments are easy for me. More often than not I can use something you have taught me. I'm enjoying doing well, but I think I might be ready for more of a challenge. Pat says just you wait – it'll get plenty challenging without me dropping hints about it.

Even though I'm enjoying the class and really like Pat, I do miss you so much. After every class I just wish and wish that I were coming home to you – to Whittington Moor, because that's where I always think of us – where we'd sit at the kitchen table (me on the yellow chair as always and you on the red one) and we'd have a pot of tea and talk about what I've learned that day. Though actually, if we were still at Whittington Moor I wouldn't be up here, taking a class at the College. I wouldn't need to – you'd teach me all I need to know about philosophy and logic. Of course, I wouldn't have met Pat either. But then I wouldn't have needed to do that either.

I'm working up my courage to ask the instructor if he knows about the Durants. (I'm 100% sure Pat doesn't – but she knows an awful lot about loads of other things. You'd be amazed. I know I am.) I think I need to know – before I ask him – how I'll be if he says he doesn't. Or even if he says he does. I hope you wouldn't be disappointed in me, Will. I haven't done much lately on our project. Somehow it's not the same without you to guide me. Oh, maybe I'm hoping the lecturer will be helpful and I'm afraid to find out he can't. Or won't. Yes, I think I need to know how I'd handle whatever he says before I risk asking him anything. I wish I knew what you'd do in the circumstances.

I wish I knew what Jack Lewis would do, too, but really I know so much less about him that I do about you that it hardly seems worth wondering. Perhaps my interest in him was what you'd call a flash-in-the-pan. Would you think so?

This is something I can't talk to Pat about. She wouldn't see any reason to not ask. She's very brave, as well as very wise. Her boyfriend Glyn is coming out of jail next week and she is so matter-of-fact about it. How I wish YOU were coming back next week. I would be anything BUT matter-of-fact. Words can't describe how much I miss you. Oh dear, I'm crying again....

•

'How come you haven't been going to your counsellor, Jessica?' Her father was obviously working at sounding nonchalant but Ariel could sense a tricky conversation looming and tensed herself in readiness.

'You knew I wasn't going – you said I didn't have to if I didn't think it was doing me any good.' She struggled to match his level tone. 'And it wasn't – it was making me worse. You

11

knew that.'

Howard sighed. 'I know, I know. I think I thought you'd just skipped a session or two though. I didn't realise you'd bunked off for good.'

'I'm not going back.' She set her lips in a tight stubborn line and put her knife and fork down. They were having breakfast and she had been enjoying the bacon and eggs Howard had cooked, but now she couldn't eat. 'Anyway, who's been talking to you about me? Have you been to a Team Meeting without me knowing?'

'I have actually. And I didn't say anything to you because I didn't think it would amount to anything other than "she's doing fine". I didn't know I was going to get attacked because you weren't keeping in touch with the Team.' He was getting agitated. Her stepmother muttered 'excuse me,' got up from the table, and left the room.

Ariel took a deep, steadying breath as she watched Ellen go, and did her best to sound calm. 'Well I am doing fine. You can see that for yourself. I'm going to college three times a week and I'm working hard on maths and things with Paul, I sometimes go birding and I've got a friend I can do so-called normal things with.' She forced herself to smile at him. 'And I've been feeling better and better since I stopped going for counselling or seeing the social workers. You can't deny that.'

'Yes, sorry Jess.' He looked a bit sheepish. 'Actually I think you're right. I suppose I just didn't like being attacked yesterday when I wasn't expecting it. You are doing better and I should have stood up for you. Okay, I'll phone the social worker and tell her. Keep it up at least till you're eighteen and then they won't have any say in who you see or what you do.' He reached over and rubbed her hand. She flinched inwardly and struggled not to pull away; she needed him to feel they were close so he'd keep the social workers and counsellors at bay. She hated how much they interfered, or tried to, in her life. Possibly he and Ellen did, too. She hadn't thought of that.

When Will had died she had been officially taken into care. Her own mother and stepfather had been deemed inadequate to look after her – after all, she'd only been picked up by Will because she'd run away from the family home – but her birth father and his new wife had eventually cleared all the necessary hurdles to become 'appropriate carers' so, a few months after her fourteenth birthday, she had begun living with them. She had thought at the time that that would be the end of the Team's involvement, but she had been wrong. Probably because she'd been living with Will for two years, they apparently felt a great need to keep a watchful eye on her and all her activities, and keep her on the At-Risk Register. Despite all her protestations – and an embarrassing physical examination – they had refused to believe that the relationship had been more father-daughter and not overtly sexual. The fact that they had planned to consummate their love for one another the very night that Will had been killed in a car crash was something she kept secret, hardly allowing even herself to acknowledge it to herself.

She was good at keeping secrets. She had told no one that Will had picked her up – had actually abducted her. She selectively remembered only that she had wanted to be with him, to go with him in the first place. Now, at fifteen and a half, she only remembered how much she loved being with him and what fabulous times they'd had together. She was rapidly forgetting how, in the last few months with him, she had gradually felt more and more sexually alive to him, to the point that on that awful fatal evening she had kissed him 'properly' on the lips and they had promised each other that they would make love that very night – even though she had not fully understood what that actually meant. Will-as-Dad was far more alive in her memory than Will as about-to-be-lover. Because a Dad was what she had so badly wanted and needed.

Not talking to anyone about their 'work' together (continuing the writings of the American philosophers Will and Ariel Durant) also came easily. She felt fairly certain nobody she knew had ever heard of the Durants, and was equally sure that no one would understand how her Will had become Will Durant (Will Dee in his case) and had bestowed the Ariel Durant (Ariel Dee) mantle on her. They had changed their birthdays to match the real Will and Ariel, and large parts of their days together had been given over to reading and writing about the couple and their goal to bring their ideas about civilization and philosophy to the common man.

After Will's death she had remained (in her eyes) semi-sane, by attempting to continue writing the next chapter in the Story of Civilization, but gradually her energy and enthusiasm had flagged. She still began each day by looking at her writings but now added hardly anything to them. Occasionally she would change a word: 'a' to 'the' for example, only to change it back the following day. As long as the computer asked her 'save changes?' when she shut the document down she felt she had done something and therefore didn't have to feel too guilty.

Or so she told herself. She actually felt horribly guilty, and that she was letting Will down and would somehow be punished for her laxity. And although the guilt seemed ever-present, rumbling along in the background of her mind, she was also shocked by how little she was now thinking about either of the Wills during most days and as she was drifting off to sleep at night.

Far more often she thought about Pat and what her new friend had confided to her that day or the day before. Pat's approach to life seemed staggeringly simple (have fun!) and her accounts of what she had been up to between classes was both fascinating and incredible to Ariel. She couldn't imagine, for example, holding a kiss for over fifteen minutes.

'How do you breathe?' she'd asked.

'We breathe each other's breath, silly.' Pat had replied loftily, clearly discouraging any further questions on that topic.

Ariel hoped, for Pat's sake, that they had both cleaned their teeth and hadn't been eating fish or garlic.

FOUR

Saturday

Dear Will,

The P&L class gets more and more interesting every week. Yesterday the lecturer (on whom Pat has a bit of a crush*, she says, even though her Glyn is now out of prison and occupying most of her time and almost all her thoughts) told us a joke to test our powers of logical thinking: This man was talking about dying and being on life support, and he said to his wife 'If I'm ever on life support and not improving, I want you to unplug me' Pause. 'Then plug me back in and see if that works'.

Between you and me, I didn't get it at first, though I pretended to, but when I finally did I thought it was very funny. I know you'd get it right away and I think you'd probably find it funny too.

You can see why I love this class -- a statement the lecturer would doubtless challenge immediately, so I'll be specific. It's the closest I've come and probably ever will come to life with you. NOT because of the lecturer; I don't really share Pat's feelings about him, though he's nice enough, but because of the way the content challenges my mind. And improves it, no doubt. And because of Pat. I've never had anybody in my life like her.

Our homework this week is the sort of question you apparently might get asked at an interview for Oxford: Is it immoral to buy a £1,000 handbag? We have to write no more than 1,000 words, which might be hard for me as I think I have a lot to say – on both sides. Pat has written 'if you want it, buy it' and insists that's all she has to say. I think she'll probably write a bit more before Tuesday though. She had written 'If you want it, buy the bloody thing', but then evidently had second thoughts. 'And reduced the word count by 25%', she said

* A crush: I'm ashamed to admit that I didn't know what she meant at first. And she knew it, which made me feel even worse.

Yesterday she asked me if I'd been locked up for five years 'because you're so naïve...'. I suppose in a way I have (not five though, maybe two) though I didn't (and don't!) see being with you as being 'locked up'. But not being with girls (or boys) my own age means I don't always know the language. I'm catching up though. You'd be surprised. I hope you'd be pleased, too. Maybe I could teach you something for a change, to reimburse you for all the big words you taught me!

You wouldn't be pleased at how little I've done on the Durants lately. I feel so guilty about that. Looking at my attempts to re-write what I've remembered of what we've done together makes me miss you so much I can hardly bear it. And I feel so inadequate to write anything useful without you. I did think how Will and Ariel would love the question about the £1,000 handbag, but can't, for the moment, think how they'd answer it. Nor Jack Lewis for that matter; he apparently hated living in the modern world (did you know he failed his driving test seventeen times?!!!). Oh I wish you were here so we could talk about it. I know you'd have something really profound to say about it that would help me organise my own thinking. It would be fun to imagine Will and Jack Lewis totally not understanding how on earth a handbag could cost £1,000. We could imagine both scenarios for Ariel Durant; that would help me write a succinct response for 'Teach' (that's what Pat calls him; his name is Mr Woods).

It's almost two whole years since you were here. (I can't write that any other way...the 'k' word.) Does it get easier? THAT ought to be a question for the Oxford entrance exam because there is very definitely a right answer: NO, it does not. I miss you so, so much and think about you day and night. Well, not quite, there's a bit of hyperbole there, but I do miss you all the time even if I'm not actively thinking about you.

●

'Glyn wants to know if you want to come out with us on Saturday night. You wouldn't be the odd one out because he'd bring his friend.' Ariel's bus had arrived just before Pat's, so she had waited to walk to class with her friend, thinking how lovely it would be if Will could see her now. He'd be pleased for her that she had a friend like Pat. Wouldn't he?

'Out where?' Ariel was shocked, thrilled and scared, so she focused on the only things that for the moment had any reality for her. 'What's his friend's name?'

'It might be Ian if he's around. Or it could be Simon I suppose. They're both fairly good looking, though I'd never say that to Glyn, of course. He can be a bit touchy about these things, my Glyn.'

'Where would we go?' As if it mattered. And Pat didn't respond anyway. 'I'll have to ask the parents though.'

In the event she didn't ask. She thought they would probably ask too many questions and might even demand to meet Ian/Simon before saying yes. She considered asking just her stepmother, feeling there would probably be more flexibility there, but at the last minute decided not to, thinking that Ellen might feel obliged to tell Howard and then they'd be back to square one. So two days later, in class, she told Pat she would come and asked again where they would be going.

'I don't know,' Pat sounded irritated, 'what does it matter? We'll just meet somewhere and see what happens. We could go for some coffee or we could go for a walk, I don't know. I just want to go out and have some fun.'

Ariel was shocked at the apparently sudden change in Pat. She'd never known her be anything other than cheerful and bright before, but before she could do more than wonder whether she should leave her alone or apologise and somehow make amends, Mr Woods arrived and launched into his own stream of consciousness that drove all other thoughts from Ariel's head.

At the end of the period Pat seemed to be more or less back to normal, so Ariel decided not to mention it. All the same, she was careful not to be annoying and left to go home much sooner than was her habit. As she walked up her road she thought that had probably been the right thing to do, but felt slightly hurt that

Pat had not seemed to notice. She soothed her discomfort as best she could by counting the number of cars coming down the road as compared to the number going in the opposite direction. As expected, as this time of day, it was almost equal. She wondered what variables she might introduce to make things more interesting. Certainly monitoring the road at different times of the day: that would make a difference.

Will had taught her that counting and keeping statistical records was a comfort, and she mentally thanked him for it. In fact, she felt such a rush of gratitude that when she got home she felt it was only right that she spent some time now working on the next chapter of the Durants' Story of Civilization.

She looked at what she had written so far. The work that she and Will had done together was gone, so she had had to try to recreate as much of what she could remember they had done together; quite unsuccessfully, as it turned out. In the beginning, she had not been able to concentrate because her anger at not being allowed to have anything from the home she and Will had shared had almost consumed her. She had asked for the books, particularly the Durants' Story of Civilization, but had not been allowed to have them. Even her own journal had been taken – for evidence against Will, she assumed – and never returned to her. All things considered, she thought she now wouldn't want that back, it would be too painful, but the anger still simmered at what she saw as sheer callousness on the part of the various authorities involved in the case. No one had told her quite what Will was supposed to have done (apart from abducting her, which was a serious enough crime, apparently) though none of them – social workers, carers, counsellors, almost without exception, had made any attempt to hide their separate and collective opinions that he was a thoroughly bad man. Actually, she told herself repeatedly, she didn't want to know. As far as she was concerned, whatever he might have done would have been done for a good reason. He was that sort of person. And as for abducting her, she stubbornly maintained to everyone, including herself, that she'd wanted to go with him.

She looked at her writings again. It was no use. He'd been the one with the profound thoughts about philosophy as seen from the Durants' point of view. She'd been his 'Josephine Ordinary', making sure that what he said and wrote was understandable to ordinary people. She couldn't take that role now because he wasn't here to share his latest thinking. Therefore how could she continue? She couldn't. 'Simple as', as Pat would say.

She felt suddenly lighter, relieved, a burden lifted. She tried to see Will in her mind's eye to see if he would approve or disapprove of this conclusion, but he wasn't there. That made her feel sad. Until quite recently she'd been able 'see' him almost at will (a phrase she liked a lot and used as frequently as possible). What would he say if he were here, she wondered, and decided he would probably tell her to leave it alone and see what happened in the next few days.

Her lighter mood returned. Good old Will. He was still with her, even if she couldn't 'see' him. She could still imagine what he'd say she should do.

She shut down the file and began thinking about what she might wear on Saturday. It would have to be something that went well with flat shoes if they were going for a walk. Which was just as well, as she didn't actually have any shoes with what might be called heels.

FIVE

Saturday

Dear Will,

Nothing much to report on W&A at the moment. It looks as if I'm taking a bit of a break – I hope you wouldn't mind too much. I suspect you'd say it's a good idea and that I'll come back to it refreshed. I hope so. On both counts (that you'd say it's a good idea and that I'll come back refreshed.

Yesterday's funny story from Mr Woods was about a statistician from Finland, demonstrating what Mr. W. called the idiocy of statistics. The Finn (I can't write statistician again!) said that the average number of legs people in his country have is 1.99recurring because there are a fair few with only one leg and also some with no legs at all. Therefore, he says, the majority of Finns have an above average number of legs! Pat and I nearly fell off our chairs laughing at first, and then were gobsmacked that at least a third of the class didn't get it! Then we felt smug.

I'm going 'out' later today, with Pat and her boyfriend Glyn and a friend of his who might be called Ian or he might be called Simon. (I'm assuming they are actually different people, but I'm not sure; I'll tell you later.) I'm sort of looking forward to it but I'm also a bit nervous. I've never met any of them except Pat and I'm not sure about her so much at the moment. I still like her a lot, of course, but she seems to be in a bad mood quite a bit, which is hard to take because she's always been so happy-go-lucky. And now I'm being really 'girlie' and worrying about what to wear. Can you imagine? We might go for a walk, so it will have to be something appropriate – the sort of thing I wear to go birding, I suppose, except none of those clothes are really 'going out' clothes.

Missing you, Will, and wondering what it would be like if you were here, helping me decide what to wear this evening. And then realising, for the 900th time, that if you were still here I wouldn't be going out this evening. Life is so strange.

•

She had arranged to meet Pat at the bus station café at seven o'clock. At half past six she realised she couldn't just walk out of the house; she had to have a reason so the parents wouldn't think it odd. She decided on the truth – or at least the partial truth.

'Is it okay if I meet Pat at the bus station café this evening?' She was dressed in her jeans and a relatively new fleece top, so felt they wouldn't suspect there was anything else afoot. 'We'd thought we'd go over our logic assignments together.'

'Oh that's nice,' Ellen was enthusiastic. 'Do you need some money for a coffee or something?' She took a ten pound note from her purse and passed it to Ariel who smiled her thanks.

'Do you want a lift to the bus station?' Howard was apparently equally unconcerned and happy for her to be doing something 'normal' for a change. She thought he might also be checking up on her to make sure that's what she was doing, but accepted the offer anyway.

It was a five-minute drive to the bus station during which he asked if she needed any more money and told her not to be out too late. 'If you need lift home, just ring me,' he said. 'Have a good time.'

She was either early or Pat and Co were late because she was the only person in the café. She bought a tea and sat where she could see the door and people approaching from either side. She didn't have long to wait.

'Are you Ariel?' a boy of about her own age, slightly taller, with hair the colour and texture of dried grass stood beside her table. 'I'm Ivor, friend of Glyn and Pat's.' He offered his hand so she shook it. His skin was rough, but his grip was limp and felt unpleasant. 'What're you drinking?'

'Hi. Yes. Tea.' She was very uncomfortable. She had not thought that she would have to meet the friend without Pat's comforting presence. And why Ivor? What had happened to Ian? And Simon? Dare she ask?

Ivor went to the counter and came back with two cups of tea and a plate of rich tea biscuits. 'Here. Not exactly champagne and caviar, but not bad for a bus station establishment.' He sat down opposite her. 'How are you anyway, Ariel?'

'Oh, fine. Thanks.' Where was Pat? This was excruciating. For something to do she ripped open a packet of sugar and stirred it into her tea, even though she normally didn't take sugar at all. That helped, so she did it again. And then a third and finally a fourth time.

'Blimey! You take a lot of sugar! I'd have spots for six weeks if I had that much.' He looked admiringly at her face. 'Your skin is lovely though.'

She tried to smile and not look as if she were waiting desperately for Pat to appear. She stirred her tea again, thought about reaching for more sugar, changed her mind and stirred her tea once more. Her fingernails found a groove on the under side of the table and she ran them back and forth in it, counting silently to herself as she did so. Ivor kept looking at her, munching biscuits and nodding solemnly as he did so.

'What time is it?' She didn't really care, but the silence was too painful.

'Dunno. Why?'

'Oh, I was just wondering where Pat was. We were supposed to meet here at seven o'clock...'

'Were you? I thought you were supposed to be meeting me. Pat and Glyn have gone to the pictures.'

'Oh.' She didn't know what else to say so said nothing and tried to absorb the information. Unfortunately he didn't say anything either, so they sat in uncomfortable silence again for several minutes.

'How do you know Glyn?' she finally thought of something to say.

'We met in prison. And now he's a rugby mate. And we both have Welsh names so I suppose it's natural that we'd pal up.

How do you know Pat then?'

'From the college. I sit next to her in Philosophy and Logic.'

'Philosophy and Logic? Blimey. That's a bit deep innit?' His lips turned downwards and he looked both disapproving and scornful.

'Oh it's all right. It can be quite funny at times.' She didn't want to seem too odd to him, but on the other hand she didn't want to sneer at what was currently one of the best things in her life. 'It's not as stuffy as it sounds, I can assure you.'

'Oh can you indeed! Personally I think you're much too pretty to be giving yourself brain ache with a class like that. Same for Pat too – what's she doing there anyway?'

Ariel didn't know, so shrugged. Obviously she and Ivor weren't going to have a discussion about her burgeoning college career, nor about philosophy and logic. She couldn't imagine at this point what else they might talk about, and wondered how soon she could reasonably say she had to go home. Especially as he had a tendency to chew the biscuits with his mouth open, allowing crumbs to fall over his chin and down onto his chest.

'Want to go for a walk?' Ivor stood up, licked his lips and brushed the biscuit crumbs off his lime green and purple striped jumper. He held out his hand to her, 'it's nice down by the river this time of an evening.'

Grateful to be doing something instead of sitting in strained and painful silence, Ariel stood up too, took his proffered hand and together they walked out of the café, across the bus station yard and down to the riverwalk path. Maybe he was interested in birds. She asked him.

'Yes, I suppose so… Oh, you mean birds! No, no way.'

They walked slowly in the growing darkness, not speaking, hand-in-hand for several hundred metres. When they had gone under a bridge and emerged to a gated field on the other side Ivor stopped and firmly pushed her against the wooden bars of the gate.

'You're quite pretty. I love your freckles. I don't usually like freckles, but yours are really sweet.' He sounded so sincere that she was moved to say 'You're handsome'. She didn't know what else to say, but thought she ought to say something else; probably something specific about his looks. Perhaps she should comment on his hair, but she couldn't think what she might say. However, before she could think of anything she felt Ivor's lips touch hers. She'd had her mouth partially open ready to speak as soon as she thought of something appropriate, so the kiss went off her lips and onto her teeth.

'Oh sorry,' she giggled nervously. How awful for Ivor to have his kiss met with her teeth, which probably weren't as clean as they might be after all that sugary tea. She half-hoped it wouldn't put him off too much and that he would try again. This is what normal people do, she told herself. She pressed her lips together to be ready this time, almost but not quite snatching the memory of the thrill she'd felt when she'd kissed Will.

'I've been wanting to do this all evening.' He pushed harder against her and the middle rail of the gate pressed painfully on her back; hopefully not, she thought, damaging her kidneys for life.

'Have you really?' She'd had to open her mouth to speak and before she could get it closed he was kissing her again. She tried to get her lips together but something was in the way. She moved her head back, but the something – it flashed across her mind that it felt like a tinned sardine and tasted of biscuit crumbs– didn't move out. It moved in! Oh crikey, it was his tongue!

She wanted to laugh. She squirmed a little and he tightened his arms around her, moving his tongue up and down inside her mouth. She tried to keep her own tongue out of the way; she wanted to make it easy for him, make plenty of room, but her jaw was beginning to ache with the effort of not closing her teeth on the wiggling thing. How could she get him to take it out? She made little noises in her throat but he seemed to take that as encouragement to stick his tongue further and further inside her mouth. Oh God! Is this what Pat and Glyn did for fifteen minutes? How could Pat stand it?

Abruptly Ivor stood back. Ariel didn't know what to do or say. Should she say thank you? She didn't have to put her tongue in his mouth now, did she? She hoped not.

'Was that your first time?'

'How did you know?' She turned her head away as she spoke so Ivor wouldn't take the opportunity to put his tongue in again as she opened her mouth to speak.

'It wasn't exactly dynamite, you know. But you'll learn. I can teach you if you like.'

'Well, not now though. I have to get home. I'm already late.' She had no idea what time it was but was perfectly willing to say she was supposed to be home by half past seven if necessary. She was suddenly desperate to be home. Maybe she and Ellen could play a game of Monopoly, or even Scrabble. Ellen wasn't very good at Scrabble so it wasn't usually much fun for Ariel. But it would be better than this, she thought. Almost anything would.

'All right, let's go then.' Ivor set off rapidly, hands in his pockets, and she hurried to keep up. Neither of them spoke until they got back to the bus station café where he simply said 'see you', and strode off before she could reply.

The bus station clock said twenty-past-eight. Was that all? It felt like hours since her father had dropped her here at five to seven. She went inside and bought another tea but couldn't drink it. She made herself wait until nine o'clock and then phoned home to ask for a lift. Waiting anxiously outside the café, she thought she'd never in her life been so glad to see anyone as she was when Howard drove up.

'Good time?'

'Uhm…okay,' airily. She didn't want to lie, but she couldn't talk to him about what had happened either. She certainly wasn't going to tell him she'd been kissed by an ex-convict. She was anxious to get home, clean her teeth and hopefully get rid of the fishy taste of Ivor's tongue. She used to quite like sardines, but knew she'd never eat them again now. And probably not biscuits for a while, either.

Later, as she was waiting rather tensely for sleep to claim

her, she fully remembered the first and only time she had kissed Will 'properly', on the lips. She didn't remember there being any tongue involved on that occasion, in fact she was pretty certain there hadn't been, but she could remember the frisson she'd felt when he had responded. Surely that's what kissing was supposed to feel like. Surely you weren't supposed to be repulsed by the other person. She wondered if she could ask Pat about it.

SIX

Sunday

Dear Will,

My evening out with Pat and Glyn's friend was a total disaster. I can't even write about it so I have no idea what you'd say about it all. I can't 'see' you in my head anymore, either, which is making me feel very sad and lonely. My brief flirtation with Jack Lewis seems to be going nowhere – he just couldn't come up to Will and Ariel and you. So much about him makes me even more sad. And Pat is still in considerably less than good humour more days than not, so not much fun to be with. I seem to be losing people all round.

I don't know what to write about at the moment. Maybe I'll go birding later. Who knows, I might see something new and/or unusual. But then, who would I tell? Who would be interested?

Oh dear, I'm feeling very sorry for myself this morning. More tears…

•

Pat wasn't in class on Tuesday, though Ariel thought she'd caught sight of her outside the cafeteria earlier. Mr Woods had asked 'where's your mate today, Ariel?' and she'd felt embarrassed that she didn't know how to answer. She never had any problem speaking up about the topics being discussed, but anything else left her almost completely tongue-tied. At the end of the session the lecturer signalled to her to wait, so she stood uncertainly beside his table, waiting until he'd finished with the two or three other students with questions for him.

'Can you let Pat know about the assignments, Ariel?'

She nodded, though she wasn't at all sure she'd know how to

contact Pat if she wasn't somewhere nearby and visible.

'Okay, thanks.' He stared at her. 'How come you go by Ariel if you're really Jessica Pike?'

She hadn't been expecting that so had no answer ready. 'Oh…well, I sort of changed my name a couple of years ago…' She knew she was blushing horribly.

'But not legally? You can do a deed poll thing for a bit of dosh, you know, and then you won't have to put up with nosy people like me asking impertinent questions.' He smiled and handed her an assignment sheet to take to Pat. 'See you tomorrow.'

A deed poll thing! What on earth was that? She would go straight home and look it up on the internet. She'd probably have to have her father's permission, maybe even the social work team's, but she'd cross that bridge if and when, she thought. Meanwhile she walked with new purpose over to the cafeteria where she found Pat drooping at an outside table. She looked awful. Ariel had read about people turning green around the gills but had never imagined a real live person could look as green-tinged as Pat did at that moment. She managed not to mention it though, somehow knowing that would be the wrong thing to focus on.

'Missed you,' she said instead, 'are you okay?' She sat down beside Pat and handed her the assignment sheet.

'Not really. Felt sick as a dog all morning and can't eat anything. It's been like this since last week.'

'Should you go to the doctor? Maybe you've got a virus or something.'

'Nah. I never get things like that. No, I'll be fine, just don't talk about it. In fact, let's get the hell out of here, I might feel better away from food smells.'

They walked slowly towards the bus stop where Pat said suddenly, 'my bus is coming. Bye.'

'See you tomorrow?'

'Hope so. Thanks for the assignment. Sometime catch me up on what I've missed today. Bye again.'

Ariel waited for her own bus and went home. So that's why Pat had been in such a bad mood – she'd been feeling ill. She desperately hoped Pat would feel better soon, but the relief that her friend hadn't 'gone off' her was tremendous. She almost skipped up the road to her house, intent on finding out about deed polls.

•

Pat was at her desk, drawing tiny intricate flowers around Glyn's name intertwined with her own, when Ariel arrived at the class next day. The relief was huge, and all the sweeter when Pat looked up and smiled a welcome.

'Feeling better?' Ariel was hopeful. After all, Pat was there, though she didn't think her friend actually looked any better. The word wan came to mind; Pat looked wan and frail, like the heroine of a Jane Austin novel somehow, and still rather green.

'Don't ask. I'm better if I don't think about my guts. Anyway, I've got a job for you if you want it.'

'A job? What sort of a job?'

'Nothing exciting, but then on the other hand, nothing too taxing either. It's babysitting for the couple who live next door to us. My mum wants me to do it but to be honest, it gets in my way of spending nice quality time with Glyn. She doesn't fully understand about Glyn, my mum, which is probably because I don't really tell her about him. I'm not sure she could cope with the whole truth and nothing but. Anyway, I've sat for the Parkers a couple of times and I have to say they pay well and treated me very nicely too. Left me a tray with some cake, a bottle of cider, and two cigarettes. And they paid me.'

'What did you have to do?'

'Nothing. Absolutely nothing at all. Just be there in case of a fire, I suppose. The kids were in bed so I did some homework and read a couple of Mrs P.'s trashy magazines and then wrote to Glyn – he was still in prison then. So what do you think?'

Ariel wasn't sure, but at least this was something she could do to help Pat. And if it was true that the children were in bed and didn't need any attention from her, then why not? So she nodded, 'Okay, I'll give it a go.'

She became aware of the silence in the room and looked up to see Mr Woods, head cocked on one side, looking expectantly at her.

'If you ladies have quite finished your doubtless rivetingly exciting exchange of gossip, perhaps you can remember that I am paid – not a lot, it has to be said – by the college, to instil some sense of mental discipline in your bone- or fluff-heads. You'll know which you are. And please also know that I have some sense of loyalty to those who pay me – pittance that it is.'

'Sorry Mr Woods,' Ariel wanted to explain that she was concerned about Pat, but knew that Pat would not want her business broadcast. So, 'I am sorry. I'm listening now.'

'Good-oh. Then tell us which quote you have chosen from Epictetus, if you please.'

'Epictetus, Greek Philosopher, "The key is to keep company only with people who uplift you, whose presence calls forth your best".' She waited anxiously for signs of his approval.

'Okay. Thank you. On the surface this is fairly simplistic, almost boring, wouldn't you say class?' A few murmured their assent. 'But actually, Ariel, this is well-chosen, simply because it seems so straightforward and who could argue with it? But your assignment – all of you – is to pick it apart, using the techniques I hope I have taught you, and find the flaws. We'll start now, in class, and you can finish it for next Tuesday if you please.'

SEVEN

Saturday

Dear Will,

Missing you more than ever and especially when it comes to assignments for the P&L class. You and I would have such pleasure in every single homework task, and especially the current one. We had to come up with a quote from a Greek philosopher. We pulled names from a pot and I got Epictetus. Of whom I had never heard, I have to say, but that doesn't daunt yours truly. What's Google for, I ask you!

I came up with 'the key is to keep company only with people who uplift you, whose presence calls forth your best'. I'd be the first to admit that I chose it because I was thinking of you and how your very presence uplifted me and – you were kind enough to say so on many occasions – that my presence did the same for you. Honestly I hadn't realised that he ('Teach' – Mr Woods) was going to get us to pick it apart. He professed himself very pleased with my choice and seemed to think I'd picked that very quote because I knew it was deeper than it seemed. He was wrong. I've just explained to you why I chose it! But...that's the assignment. Hence my missing you so terribly. I smiled knowingly at the time, but actually I'm a bit panic-stricken at the moment.

And I can't give it any attention for now anyway – I'm off to do some paid work! I'm babysitting for Pat's next door neighbours if you please. It will be nice to have a bit of money in my pocket (another reason to miss you – the parents give me 'pocket money' in minuscule amounts and want a fairly specific accounting of how I spend it. But when I run out, I only have to ask and they nearly always give me more. Your budgeting soul would cringe, methinks. But anyway, mostly I'm doing it to help Pat out. She'd rather spend time with her Glyn and as she's feeling definitely under the weather these days, I'm glad to help make that possible. I only hope it won't be another ghastly mistake – the first one being Ivor. (Which I still haven't written about.)

Somehow 'Nanny Ariel' doesn't have a good ring to it...But you never know.

•

Pat had told her which bus to catch from the bus station. 'I'll meet you off the seven o'clock bus. Ask the driver to stop for you at the Slug and Lettuce. It's the stop after the big shopping centre so you'll know when you're nearly there.'

But Pat wasn't there. Ariel stood for a moment or two, wondering how she could tell which house was Pat's and therefore which, next door, was the Parkers. She tried not to think that something had happened to Pat, that she was feeling worse, but it was easier to think that than to assume she'd simply forgotten and didn't care.

'For heaven's sake,' she thought, 'Don't be such a wimp. You managed to get yourself from Sheringham to Will's house in Whittington; you can surely find Pat's house or the Parkers.' She straightened her shoulders and looked around. She didn't know Pat's last name, she suddenly realised; Mr Woods no longer called out full names at the start of class and she hadn't paid attention at the beginning of the term. But she did know she was expected at the Parkers. Surely they would be known to the owners of the Slug and Lettuce.

They were. 'Last but one house on the left, on Coppice Drive,' said the cheery young man behind the bar. 'About five minutes' walk.'

Pleased with her resourcefulness and the ease with which she had followed the directions, Ariel rang the doorbell with confidence. A pleasant-looking and slightly plump woman answered almost immediately.

'Hello! You must be Ariel. Do come in, I'm Joy Parker, and this,' looking around, 'is my husband, Clive.' She shook Ariel's hand and Clive then did the same. 'I'll show you where the boys are – they're sound asleep and absolutely guaranteed not to wake up. But if they do, just ring us – here's the number, speed-dial two – and we'll come straight home. We aren't far away, just at the shopping centre cinema. We'll be back by eleven anyway and Clive will drive you home.'

She led the way upstairs where Ariel cast a quick glance at the sleeping children, nodded (confidently, she hoped) and followed Joy back downstairs where Clive was zipping up his jacket. 'We're off then. Please don't hesitate to ring us if you need to about anything. We're so grateful you could do this.' And they were gone.

Less than a minute later Joy returned. 'Oops, completely forgot to show you where the downstairs loo is. It's there,' pointing to a door, 'and please feel free to explore the rest of the house so you know where things are, like the kitchen.' The couple left again, leaving Ariel to look around by herself.

The promised tray was there, on the table. A generous slice of what could only be a home-made cake in cling film, a Terry's Chocolate Orange, a banana, a bottle of pear cider and two cigarettes. Ariel shook her head in wonderment. She'd never in her life smoked a cigarette nor, as far as she knew, had anything alcoholic to drink. She thought she might like to try the pear cider, but she'd leave the cigarettes. Unless she took them for Pat; for all she knew Pat – or Glyn – would appreciate them. She wondered who the smoker in this house was; there was no smell of cigarette smoke so perhaps it was Mr Parker and he only smoked at work. If he was allowed to. She wondered what he did for a living.

She had brought her class notes with her, intending to use the time to write her analysis of the seemingly innocuous Epictetus quote. Why oh why had she chosen that one? What could possibly be wrong with it anyway? She pondered a while, absent-mindedly eating first the banana and then the cake. What would Will say? What would Jack Lewis say? 'Actually, not a lot. They're both dead,' she was surprised to hear herself say out loud. Crikey, was that the first time she'd really acknowledged Will's death? She thought about that for a while, giving way to some gentler tears than she'd cried before when thinking about

Will's absence.

She was startled to hear the front door bell. Perhaps it was Pat, she thought, coming to apologise for not meeting her off the bus. She blew her nose, wiped her face on her sleeve and flung open the door to be forgiving and welcoming to her friend.

'Oh, hello. Is Mrs Parker out?' He could only be described as tall, dark and handsome, and not – she was quick to observe – terribly old. And with a smile to light up Newcastle.

'Yes, she are, I mean they is…I mean…'

'I was afraid they would be. I know they like to go to the cinema on Saturdays when they can. But I thought I'd take a chance as I was in the neighbourhood. I'm Patrick, by the way, Joy's brother. Would you mind if I came in and left a note?'

'Oh no, yes I mean, please come in.' Cursing herself for being so bumbling and aware that she was tear-stained and probably also covered in cake crumbs, she fled to the bathroom to compose herself. When she returned he was sitting at the table, writing his note. He smiled at her again and picked up her notebook.

'Ariel Dee – is that you?'

She nodded, desperately wanting him to leave and equally desperately wanting him to stay. 'Would you like some of this chocolate orange?'

'I'd love some, if I'm not robbing you. Chocolate is a necessity I always think when you're doing homework. But I'll bet I can find us some more. I know where Joy keeps the goodies for grownups.'

He stayed for about forty-five minutes, drinking the cider and sharing the chocolate and expressing great interest in her P&L assignment. 'Consider the possibility that there is actually nothing wrong with the quote and your instructor is testing you. But on the other hand, I think it's fair to say that we don't grow, emotionally, if we only ever hang out with people we like being with. It makes life too easy. You're frowning – am I missing the point?'

'Nooo,' she said slowly, 'I'm just remembering a poem I

read years ago that I think was saying you have to hang out with those like you. It was by Walt Whitman and it went something like "only themselves understand themselves and the likes of themselves". Not quite the same thing, I suppose.'

'Even so, you could include it in your answer; it shows you're getting the hang of this critical thinking lark.'

She felt her excitement rise. 'Yes! And "the key", he says, the key to what? '

'Exactly! Now you're thinking analytically. You're starting to ask questions instead of just accepting what the man said. Well done! Can you do it from here, do you think?'

'Yes, I think I can. I need to ponder on it some more, but I feel much better, as if I know how to think critically about it now. Thank you so much!'

'The pleasure was all mine, I assure you.' Again the amazing smile. 'Do you babysit for Joy and Clive often?'

'This is my first time, so I don't know. I'd like to. I like them, though I've only just met them.'

'Well I may see you again then. I know they like to go out on Saturdays. Thanks for sharing the chocolate and cider.'

Ariel couldn't settle when he'd gone. She was excited about the assignment, getting a handle on how to write it, but there was more to it than that. She was unsettled by Patrick. She hoped she'd see him again, but she also hoped she wouldn't. Why would he come again if he knew his sister was out? Or is that what he meant? Maybe he wouldn't be coming again on Saturdays because he knew they'd be out. Yet he'd said he might see her again. She wondered what he did for a living. She'd ask Pat. In fact, Pat might be quite impressed by the account of Ariel's first babysitting experience; might now even be ready overlook Ariel's 'total fucking failure', said with such scorn, with Ivor.

EIGHT

Sunday

Dear Will,

She crossed it out and closed her journal. Somehow she didn't feel like writing to Will at the moment. Anyway, it was Sunday now and she'd written yesterday.

She went back to her essay on the Epictetus quote, hoping this would evoke Will in her head, but instead it was Patrick whose face appeared in her mind's eye. After two or three unsuccessful attempts to vanquish him she slammed her book shut and flopped onto the bed in exasperation.

She didn't want to tell Will, via her journal, about Patrick, but she did want to tell Pat. She knew Pat's phone number but had so far resisted ringing her, not being sure what reaction she would get, nor how to initiate the sort of conversation she was longing for. In any case, she didn't really know how she felt about it all, so she didn't know quite what she wanted to say about it either. Nor did she know how Pat was feeling and why she hadn't met Ariel off the bus as promised.

She went back to her notebook and saw that she had actually written Patrick in the margin. Crikey! When had she done that? But it was nice to see it there. What if she drew some flowers round it, like Pat does for Glyn's name? Did Pat get some comfort and pleasure from that, she wondered? Would she, Ariel? Probably not, and in any case she didn't have Pat's artistic flare. She turned the page and began her essay again.

•

On Monday, after Paul left, she Googled 'change your name by deed poll', having been distracted by Howard's apparent need to chat about her college class when she'd planned to do that originally. Only ten pounds but, as she'd expected, she wouldn't be able to do it until she was sixteen. The parents could do it for her, but she wasn't going to ask them. They were sure to say no. She would wait six months and if she still wanted to do it, she would then.

If she still wanted to do it? Where did that come from? Of course she'd still want to do it. She'd been Ariel Dee since she was twelve and had hated being made to go back to Jessica Pike when Will had been killed and she'd been first in care and then sent to live with her birth father and his newish wife. In her mind she was still Ariel and she couldn't see that changing.

She wondered what Patrick's last name was and hardly noticed she'd thought 'killed' in relation to Will's death. Pat would know Patrick's last name. She wondered again how Pat was, and if she'd be in class on Tuesday.

•

Pat was not there. Ariel was so worried that she almost missed handing in her assignment. Fortunately Mr Woods asked her where it was just as she was leaving. She would have been mortified if she'd gone without turning it in. Especially as she felt she'd done a good job with it after all. Thanks to Patrick.

She went to the cafeteria, hoping against hope that Pat would be there, but drew a blank. Now thoroughly rattled, she walked slowly over to the bus stop and when the number 32 bus came, Pat's bus, she made a sudden decision and got on. Anxiously watching for first the shopping centre and then the Slug and Lettuce, she wondered what on earth she was going to say when she got to Pat's house – even assuming she could find it.

Pat's mother answered the door (she'd guessed correctly which 'next door' house was Pat's) and in response to Ariel's 'I was wondering how Pat is…I'm her friend Ariel,' said ' She's a bit better this afternoon dear, but she's been very sick all morning.' Pat's mother didn't seem terribly concerned, much to Ariel's relief. 'I think she's sleeping now, but perhaps you could come over tomorrow to see her?'

With the cloud of anxiety about Pat greatly lifted, Ariel gave in to her feelings of excitement that she would be babysitting for the Parkers again on Saturday and that she might see Patrick again. Briefly she wondered how she had allowed Pat to become so important to her; she'd known her such a short time, but somehow she connected Pat with the important recent changes in her life – her return to sanity, she thought with some surprise. Meeting Pat had coincided with significantly new directions and her altered outlook; and that was before she'd even met Patrick. Oh, was this what Pat would say was having a crush on someone? Could she have a crush on Patrick so quickly? She'd ask Pat tomorrow. How interesting that they practically had the same name, too. That must mean something.

'Patrick and Pat, Patrick and Pat' she sing-songed to herself as the bus took her back to the college where she would catch the bus that would take her home. She'd have to find out if there were more direct buses between their two houses. It was ridiculous to go all the way into town just to go all the way out again.

•

Pat was sitting up in bed looking very pale when Ariel went to see her after class on Wednesday, but was obviously in good spirits and seemed pleased when Ariel said that she'd told Mr Woods that Pat was ill but getting better. She didn't mention how proud she'd felt at having inside knowledge about her friend. Pat was also very encouraging about Patrick. She listened admiringly to Ariel's account of their meeting – an account that obviously went some way towards erasing Pat's recent horror and undisguised disapproval at how Ariel had handled the Ivor situation, even though Ariel hadn't given her all the details. Maybe that was why Pat had been so scornful of her actually. But on the other hand, maybe kissing – like that – was what she and Glyn did all the time, so finding out how badly Ariel had handled it with Ivor would only intensify Pat's scorn. For all Ariel knew, Pat – normal people – actually enjoyed it.

'Are you coming back on Friday?' She'd missed her friend horribly.

'Oh yes, I'm fine now. Got the curse – floodsville, of course – but I'm not feeling sick any more'.

'What do you think was wrong? Just the curse?' Ariel had never heard it called that, but somehow knew what Pat was referring to. Nor had she ever thought of it in those terms herself. Will had been so sweet at her first time and they had celebrated together her entry into adulthood with great enthusiasm. After she'd got over the shock of finding herself bleeding, that is. She'd thought she was dying and poor Will had had to explain to her about periods and menstruation. Another way in which her almost unbelievably ineffectual mother had failed her, she thought now.

'Don't know. But I'm feeling better now, so I'll assume that's all it was. Tell me more about your Patrick besides being tall, dark and handsome. Before I fell in love with Glyn I'd always wanted a tall, dark and handsome, cynical and disillusioned Portuguese Count. I wouldn't mind one now actually, on the side.' They both giggled, and Ariel, thus encouraged and much relieved, prattled on about 'her' Patrick and what she'd felt about him.

Pat's mother brought them some sandwiches and mugs of tea, and said she was going shopping. 'Stay for tea and a bit longer Ariel, if you like. Pat's much better.'

Flushed with happiness and relief, Ariel settled on the end of Pat's bed, ready to continue her monologue. 'Does having a crush mean you might be falling in love? Is that how it goes? And then you might not mind anything – even, eventually, letting them see you naked? You know, without your bra.'

Pat didn't answer and Ariel became aware of an acute change in the atmosphere. She looked at her friend. 'What?'

'Can you keep a secret? I mean a real one, never, never, ever to be told to anyone?'

'Of course.' She meant it. Pat was so solemn she knew this

was important and she felt tremendously proud to be so trusted.

'Well Glyn's already seen me naked.'

Ariel didn't know how to answer so she nodded gravely and hoped Pat would continue.

'All over, actually. And then some.'

Ariel felt her eyes grow bigger as she realised what Pat was probably telling her. 'Then some what? I mean…did you…did he…?

Pat sat up straighter. 'Open that drawer – the middle one.'

Ariel got off the bed and pulled open the drawer. Pat's huge collection of tops and jumpers nestled, higgledy-piggledy, inside. She struggled not to ask why Pat hadn't made neat piles as Will had taught her to do, always putting the clean or new items under what was already in the drawer.

'Look under the blue one.'

It was an empty bottle, a medicine bottle. Ariel picked it up and looked at Pat, not understanding, and surreptitiously trying to tidy the clothes into neat stacks.

'Glyn got it from a friend of his. It's supposed to bring on the curse, but I thought it was never going to work.'

Ariel abandoned the jumper-tidying and sat down abruptly. She didn't know how she knew what Pat was referring to, but somehow she did know, without any doubt. 'You mean you thought you were pre…?'

'Yes.' Pat looked like stone, then suddenly her face crumpled and huge shiny tears rolled down her cheeks. Ariel was momentarily irritated; when she cried, she looked anything but gorgeously pathetic, as Pat looked now.

'It was terrible, Ariel. You can't imagine how terrible. I've had so many hot baths and drunk so much gin I thought I'd die. Then Glyn got the idea that violent exercise would bring it on so we went up Swathe Hill and he made me run up and down the top slope over and over again. Then when I just couldn't anymore he made me drink a whole bottle of gin. I was so sick, all over his car. Even my false tooth came out and he had to feel around in the sick to get it.'

'That's true love, Pat,' Ariel didn't know what else to say. She hadn't known Pat had a false tooth, either. She wondered which one it was.

'Well then he got the medicine and yesterday the curse finally came, so it's all right now. But don't you ever mention it again. All right?'

'Oh I promise. I promise.'

'And be careful. What if the medicine hadn't worked? I don't think you can count on it, so you and Patrick thingamabob be careful.'

'Oh I will, I will.' Thank god it was only Wednesday and there was no possibility of her seeing Patrick before Saturday. If then. Crikey, what if the medicine hadn't worked and Pat had actually had a baby. She was only sixteen, only a few months older than Ariel. You couldn't get pregnant from somebody sticking their tongue in your mouth, could you? Oh god... what if...

She was on the bus home (Pat's mother told her that the number 80 was her best bet, would take her past the end of her road) hoping to persuade Ellen to play Scrabble or Monopoly with her, before she realised she hadn't asked Pat if she knew Patrick's last name.

NINE

Saturday

Do people actually write 'Dear Journal'? I don't think I will want to.

Babysitting again tonight. Do I want Patrick to show up? I think I do. After all, he can't get me pregnant without my cooperation. But at least I've Googled pregnancy and am pretty sure you can't get pregnant from somebody's tongue. Not in your mouth, anyway. I feel quite stupid for not already knowing that, actually.

So nice to have Pat back in class. And we both got A for our Epictetus analysis, though hers was totally different from mine. That's the lovely thing about this class – there aren't any absolutely right or absolutely wrong answers. In a funny kind of way, Pat was spot-on from the very first when she said it was a trick question. Come to think of it, Patrick was saying something quite similar last week when we discussed the quote and whether it was worth questioning. In the end I left out the Walt Whitman bit; I couldn't work out where I was going with it. Sometimes I get tangled up in what Pat calls my fancy words and concepts. I hadn't fully realised until I started the P&L class that Will had taught me an enormous number of words that most people my age don't use. Or possibly even know.

I wonder what Patrick's last name is. For that matter, I wonder what Pat's last name is. I shall ask her both on Tuesday. I know Glyn's last name is Owen because Pat sometimes writes 'Pat and Glyn Owen', or sometimes just 'Pat Owen' in her notebook and then draws lovely flowers round it.

●

Joy Parker greeted her like an old friend when she arrived for her babysitting assignment. 'It's such a relief to know everything is under control so we can relax and enjoy the film. My brother said he really enjoyed meeting you – and nicking my last chocolate orange! He's always been like that though. Taking my chocolate, I mean, not fulsomely praising everyone he meets.' She paused for a quick breath. 'Okay, don't forget you can phone us if you need to. See you about eleven. Bye.'

Ariel waited to make sure they had really gone, then went upstairs to make sure the boys were safely asleep. They looked so sweet and innocent; the older one on his back with his mouth slightly open and the little one with his starfish hands splayed out on the blanket. She gently picked up one small hand and was astonished at how soft and warm it felt. Goodness! Don't tell me I'm getting all maternal, she thought as she gently tucked the hand inside the covers, and then broke into a smile as it snaked back out and onto the exact same spot on the blanket as before.

Downstairs again she thought she could have peeked into Joy and Clive's bedroom, but somehow didn't feel she should. She looked at her tray for the evening: Pear cider again, two small plums, a slice of what looked like treacle tart, and a bar of chocolate. No cigarettes. Of course – she'd forgotten last week to take them for Pat and Glyn, so the Parkers would have realised she didn't smoke. Oh well, no great loss.

She looked at her class notebook. There was no assignment this week for some reason, so she re-read her notes from earlier. She looked at the clock: twenty-five past eight. Would there be anything on television she might want to watch? The Parkers seemed to have the same satellite system as the parents, so she deftly flicked through the channels and came up with nothing to hold her interest. She should have brought a book to read. Twenty to nine. More than two hours before they came home and she could go.

He wasn't coming, was he? So the careful choosing of her clothes for the evening and the unusual attention she'd paid to her hair was not just wasted, it was stupid. As was bringing her class notebook in case Patrick was interested in any of that. She felt angry with herself. Why would he come anyway? He'd know his sister was going out now they'd got a regular Saturday night sitter. Probably everybody in their right mind or not just totally hopeless would be out on a Saturday night. What on earth did that say about her?

Five past nine. Maybe she should try to sleep, but perhaps that wasn't okay if you're babysitting. Besides, she didn't feel calm enough.

She went back upstairs and spent several minutes watching the boys sleep in the soft glow of their nightlight. That was quite soothing, so when she eventually went back downstairs she was able to pick up and flip through a cooking magazine that Joy had left on the table.

She'd enjoyed cooking for Will and had surprised herself at becoming quite good at it, especially when some creativity was called for. To her delight she found a feature in the magazine that listed five or six ingredients and asked the reader to devise a recipe by using them. She had done that when she and Will had been staying on the Isle of Skye. During their last two or three days there she'd had to use up the various things they'd accumulated over the weeks and she'd invented some pretty tasty casseroles. She got a pencil and began creating menus for her and Will in the back of her class notebook.

It wasn't until she was finally home and in bed that she realised with horror that the menus could not be for her and Will. He was dead. But in her mind she'd mixed him up with Patrick, she supposed.

She lay on her back and wondered what it would be like to be young Graham Parker, then turned onto her front and put her hands out like little Nigel. It must be nice to be part of that family, she thought. And not have to worry if your best (only!) friend still liked you a lot or if a man you'd only just met would like to see you again.

•

'Telephone for you, Jessica' Ellen called up the stairs.

'Who is it?' Ariel was suspicious. The only phone calls she got were from social workers or counsellors, none of whom she wanted to speak to at the moment. Or ever, actually.

'A Mrs Parker – isn't that the lady you babysit for?'

'Oh, yes!' She leapt off her bed and took the stairs two at a time to get to the phone. 'Hello?'

'Hi Ariel, hope I'm not disturbing you, but I was wondering if you could come a bit early this week. Clive has to work late and I'd like to do a bit of shopping before I meet him at the cinema, so why don't you come for tea? Say about 5 o'clock? Of course we'll pay you for the extra time.'

She agreed immediately. Tea with Joy Parker and the two little boys suddenly had great appeal. She wanted to get to know that family better.

•

'What's your last name, Pat?' She'd waited at the bus stop so she could walk to class with her friend. Doing this, as well as thinking about doing it, not to mention imagining Will seeing her do this, gave her enormous pleasure and often soothed her enough to fall asleep fairly easily.

'Owen'

'Owen? I thought that was Glyn's last name.'

'It is. We have the same last name, though we aren't related – as far as we know. Weird, innit?'

'Uhm. I suppose so. Do you know Patrick's last name?'

'Patrick who? Why are you looking at me like that? Oh, Mrs Parker's brother? Nope, no idea. Why?'

The question surprised Ariel. She'd assumed Pat would understand without being told what Ariel's interest in him was. She was also slightly, ever so slightly, hurt that Pat hadn't realised instantly who she was talking about. 'Oh, just wondered…'

'So ask him. Assuming he comes round again when you're there, of course. With men you never know, do you?'

There didn't seem to be an answer for that, so Ariel just shrugged and felt her happy mood evaporate. Before she could think about it though, they were in the classroom and Mr Woods was in full flow. She gave herself up to the pleasure of his lecture and didn't allow herself to think about Pat, Will, or Patrick. It was a bit of an effort, but somehow she managed it.

After class, telling herself she might be getting on Pat's nerves, though she couldn't really see why, she left quickly without waiting for her friend.

'Hold the boat!' Pat hurried after her, much to Ariel's relief; she knew she'd been testing her. 'I want to ask you something.'

'Ask away.' Ariel was so happy again she would have told Pat just about anything.

'Talking about names reminded me I keep meaning to ask you about yours. Why are you in the register as Jessica Pike if we all call you Ariel something else?'

Ariel hadn't expected that. Yet she wanted to tell Pat the whole story – or at least most of it. She was fairly sure that Pat would be interested, not shocked, and almost certainly sympathetic. Though she might not understand about the father bit. She took a long breath; this seemed like a good enough opportunity. 'It's a bit complicated actually. Have you ever heard of Will and Ariel Durant?'

Pat shook her head. 'Should I have?'

'Not really. A few years ago I met this man who was obsessed with them. They're a married couple, Americans, who wrote about philosophy and civilization and wanted to make it all available to ordinary people. In a way you could say he abducted me to help him, but I absolutely wanted to be with him, so I don't see it that way.' She stopped, looking at Pat to gauge her reaction. Her friend was looking back at her, eyes wide, intent and interested.

'Go on.'

Reassured, Ariel continued, 'He'd changed his name to Will

Dee (after Will Durant) and when I was eleven (only I was actually twelve but we didn't know that) he changed my name to Ariel Dee, so we could be like Will and Ariel Durant. He'd changed his birthday to be the same day as Will Durant's and then changed mine to be the same as Ariel Durant. We even adopted two kittens and called them Ethel and Louis, like the Durants had called their children.'

'Ethel and Louis? What kind of horrible name is Ethel for your kid! Sorry. Go on, I'm fascinated really. What happened?'

'Well, we worked on writing more things like the Durants, continuing their work, and…oh…I dunno, it was all going well when it suddenly all went wrong because I told the postman he was my dad and he panicked and made us leave and when he went to get our cats so we could take them with us he was killed in a car crash.' She was out of breath with the effort of getting it all out.

'Oh fucking hell Ariel! I knew there was something dark in your past but that's AWFUL. Bloody hell. I'm speechless. Is he the older man you kissed then?'

'Yes. I think we were going to be like husband and wife that night, but…he was killed and all hell broke loose as they say. I've never had the whole story, but it seems he was wanted by the police for something, but not just for abducting me. In any case, he didn't – I wanted to go with him. I loved him, Pat. I truly did.'

They were sitting in their usual spot under the tree between the bus stop and the cafeteria, another scene Ariel liked reviewing in her mind's eye and imagining Will looking approvingly down on them there. She glanced over at Pat. 'But truthfully I loved him more as my Dad than wanting him to be a husband. Though I know that's what he wanted…' she trailed off. 'I'm not sure you could understand that…'

'What did you mean you thought you were eleven but you were really twelve? I don't get that.'

Half-grateful for the somewhat abrupt change of focus, Ariel took another deep breath. 'Evidently my scatterbrained mother had told the school I was four when I was actually five. Then when I was missing – "presumed dead", as they say – my birth certificate emerged and Will read about it in the paper.'

'In the paper? Were you in the paper for being abducted?' Pat was clearly impressed. Ariel had never seen her eyes so large.

'Well, yes. That's what happens.' Ariel was suddenly exhausted. 'I don't want to talk about it anymore. Sorry, Pat.'

'Well blow me over...Okay, I won't go on about it.' She reached over and squeezed Ariel's hand. 'You are a dark horse though. Which is why I took to you straight away, probably. There's very definitely more in you than meets the eye. I'm glad you came and sat by me on that first day.'

Ariel attempted a smile, and shrugged – a gesture she seemed to be using rather a lot these days, she thought. Was she relieved to have told Pat or was it going to make her feel even worse? She would have liked Pat to have said she understood about Ariel's greater need for a dad than a lover, but didn't feel she could bring that up again. She thought she wanted to go home and write in her journal to Will, but almost immediately realised that actually she just wanted to go on sitting on the grass, on 'their' spot, with Pat.

Pat was looking curiously at her. 'Can I just say one thing about it? It's not a question about what you said – it's about your name.'

Ariel nodded.

'Do you actually like the name Ariel? It's a flipping washing powder you know. Not to mention Disney's Little Mermaid. Personally I'd prefer to be called Jessica and would go by Jecca. I hate my name. Glyn calls me Trisha. Actually he calls me 'dishy-Trishy', or DeeTee for short, which is like our secret code.'

On somewhat safer ground again, Ariel felt slightly better. 'Oh, I don't really know now. Will gave me that name so I loved it, but I quite like the idea of Jecca. I wonder if it's too late to start being that... I didn't want to go back to being Jessica Pike but that's who I have to be for most of the people in my life now. When I'm sixteen I can change my name legally apparently.'

'Well think about it. And let me know. Oh, I know – if you like I'll start calling you Jecca so you can test-drive it for a bit and see how you feel.'

'Okay. Thanks. Not yet though. Do you want me to call you Trisha?'

'Don't really care. Oops, here comes my bus, bye.'

TEN

Saturday

Dear Will,

You're on mind very much at the moment. Yesterday I told Pat (who likes to go by Trisha, though I'm not sure if she wants me to call her that) some of our story. It wasn't as hard as I'd imagined it would be – perhaps because it just seemed to happen so I hadn't had hours or days to get worked up about it. I had to play down some of the details – like the permanent difference in what you wanted and what I wanted. And probably needed: As in, A Dad. Pat (Trisha – I'm trying to get used to that just in case) goes for the romantic angle and I can tell would never understand about my wanting you to be my Dad. (Come to think of it, you never really understood that, either, did you?) In fact, I did mention that to her a long time ago (as you'll know if you are indeed 'looking down' on me) and she was quite shocked at that. She has a dad; he's just sort of there and she never has to think about him. I had a father who left, then the pervert step father Jock and then you, sort of. But you didn't want that, did you? You wanted something else. I always knew that, but tried to hide it from myself.

I'm sorry I keep banging on about your 'watching over me'. I know you didn't believe in any kind of after life, so of course I followed your lead in that and couldn't/wouldn't believe in it either. But at the moment I want to think differently about it. Perhaps I need to think differently from you about a lot of things, for a change. And wouldn't that be a change! The idea quite terrifies me, as a matter of fact. Anyway, oddly, it helps to think of you being 'on the other side' and looking down on me. Approvingly, I hope, or at least benignly.

Please don't think I'm 'getting religion'. I'm not. At least, I don't think I am. Though as I wrote that I thought I'd quite like to re-read Jack Lewis's Surprised by Joy to see if I can be 'surprised' like him. I sometimes feel quite connected with him. He was always looking for a mother, apparently, and I had (still have?) a similar need to find a father. I wish he were still alive and at Oxford so I could go and see him to talk about this.

But he's not. And nor are you. And my real father, with whom I actually live now, doesn't seem to even be on my radar as a dad.

Pat/Trisha doesn't think much of the name Ariel. I never liked Jessie – or Jessica, but I do like her suggestion of Jecca. I think I do, anyway.

Did you 'call forth my best', do you think? I've always believed you did. I SO want to go on believing that.

•

Tea with Joy Parker and the two little boys was even more enjoyable than she'd imagined. She was surprised by how much she enjoyed playing and interacting with Graham and Nigel and how much they seemed to like her, and was quite sorry when Joy swooped them off for a bath, a story and bed. To show her gratitude, she cleared the table and did the washing up while they were busy upstairs.

'Oh, you lovely angel!' Joy was obviously delighted with the gesture. 'Let's have a glass of wine and relax for a few minutes before I go shopping.

'I'm not sure I should drink wine actually. I'm not even sixteen yet.' Ariel was nervous about this. She'd had a sip of two of the pear cider on her second babysitting evening, waiting for Patrick, but hadn't enjoyed it. She'd never had wine in her life.

'Well I'll have wine and you can have another cup of tea then. I don't want to corrupt you.' Joy smiled reassuringly. 'It's the relax-and-chat bit I think we need anyway.' She disappeared to the kitchen and returned within minutes with a glass of wine for herself and a mug of tea for Ariel. 'Cheers! Phew, I love my sons to bits but I'm never sorry to come to the end of the day with them and tuck them safely into their beds.'

'They're very good. Not that I have any experience with

small children.' Ariel cast around for something to say that might be appropriate.

'Well yes, they are. I know that really and I'm grateful.' Joy sipped her wine. 'Are you looking forward to having children of your own, Ariel? You seem to be very good with my little ones.'

'Gosh I don't know. I haven't even thought about it.'

'Do you have a boy friend? Patrick – my brother – thought you were quite lovely, you know. Oh my goodness, I've made you blush. But he's right. I'd kill for hair like yours – when I use a red rinse I look as if I've dipped my head in beetroot juice. And you're so nice and slim, too. So what do you think of Patrick? Is there any hope?'

Ariel didn't know how to respond. She sipped her tea and tried to absorb what was, after all, just the information she'd wanted: Patrick liked her, even wondered if she were available, if she'd understood Joy correctly. 'Surprised by Joy,' she blurted out, much to her own, as well as Joy Parker's obvious astonishment.

'Oh! Really? Well, he'll probably come round later anyway. So I'll just mind my own business.' Joy finished her wine and got to her feet. 'Okay, I'm off then. Oops, I haven't done a tray for you – can you help yourself to anything you want? Nothing's off-limits as far as we're concerned.'

Ariel waited a full ten minutes after the door banged behind Joy before she went slowly into the bathroom to stare at herself in the mirror. 'Quite lovely,' he'd said. Or at least that's how Joy had interpreted whatever he had in fact said. (Mr Woods had evidently been successful in getting her to think more critically and not take things at face value, she thought.) And had he admired her hair or was that just Joy, whose own hair could only be described as mousey brown and no particular style. And he was 'probably' coming round later. Oh dear. What would they talk about? She wished she'd brought a toothbrush with her so she could clean her teeth.

She squeezed some of the toothpaste she assumed was Joy's onto her finger and rubbed it round her teeth before rinsing as vigorously as she could. That would have to do. She looked critically at her hair. She didn't think of it as red. It certainly wasn't ginger-red; more mahogany-coloured. How had it looked two weeks ago when Patrick had first seen her? Probably pretty much the same as it looked now: thick and wavy and bouncing just above her collar. She pushed it behind her ears to see if she looked more sophisticated. Not really. In any case it would never stay there. She shook her head and sure enough, it all rebounded to where it usually hung. Was it 'lovely'? She'd never thought so. She tried to remember if Will had ever said anything about it. Or about her freckles, for that matter, which Ivor had admired. Or at least, he'd said he liked them; she wasn't at all sure now of his sincerity and suspected he'd only said those nice things so she'd let him kiss her.

The doorbell made her jump. Crikey, she wasn't ready! Maybe she wouldn't answer it and he'd go away. But what if he didn't come back later? And worse – what if he told Joy there'd been nobody home when she was supposed to be looking after Graham and Nigel?

And maybe it wasn't Patrick at the door anyway. She went to answer it, doing her best to look casual and confident.

But it was Patrick, proffering a tin of toffees. 'Hello again. Thought it only fair if I brought something to share this time, having partaken of your treats the other night.' He sat at the table and began stripping the cellophane off the toffee tin. 'Hope you like toffee. This is a mixed lot so we both ought to be able to find something we like. And if not, well – as I said, I know where Joy keeps all the good stuff; we'll raid her tuck box again.'

Ariel felt herself relax immediately. He was so easy to be with and apparently didn't find it hard to keep a flow of conversation going so there weren't any awkward silences. She unwrapped a treacle toffee and thought that if she didn't know what to say she could always point to her mouth to indicate she needed to chew for a bit.

In the event she didn't need to. He didn't really ask questions except to enquire how her Epictetus essay had gone, and seemed genuinely interested when she told him what she had written. He was very admiring of her A mark and confessed that although he had really enjoyed philosophy as a subject, he'd never got more than a B+ and that only once.

'I expect my A was a fluke,' she demurred, 'beginner's luck.'

'I don't think so, Ariel. I think you demonstrate a fine grasp of it all and a superbly logical mind in such matters. And I have a hunch you know how to be frivolous, too, when the occasion warrants it.'

Not wanting to discuss herself any more and slightly amazed at her own boldness, she asked 'What sort of things do you like to do for frivolity?' but was almost too dizzy to take in much of his response. There was something about golf and tennis, and something else about a book club and chess, and finally something about playing cricket for his local village eleven.

'Maybe you'd like to come along some Sunday next summer – are you a cricket fan?'

She was indeed. And delighted to be able to talk at length with him about how Twenty20 cricket was changing the game, how well England had been doing and how things were changing with the Australians and the Sri Lankans. A temporary state of affairs, they both thought. She was amazed when, at five to eleven, Joy and Clive reappeared and her babysitting duty was over. She half-thought – and certainly hoped – that Patrick might take her home but evidently the thought hadn't occurred to Clive and he was rattling his car keys and getting her coat before there was an opportunity for any other outcome.

ELEVEN

Sunday

So much to write about and feeling much too unsettled to concentrate on writing it. Patrick did come while I was babysitting and I actually enjoyed myself with him. He seems to like many of the same things I like. Cricket, for starters. And before that (Patrick's arrival – and I still don't know his last name) I thoroughly enjoyed having tea with Joy and the boys. And finally, when Clive drove me home, he said something about all of us going to London for the day to see a show! I'm not sure quite who 'all of us' is. I shouldn't think it includes Graham and Nigel, but if not, who will be taking care of them? Oh, perhaps they're taking me along to help look after them; I hadn't thought of that. Anyway, Clive said that he or Joy would get in touch with the parents to make sure they are comfortable with whatever the arrangements are. I was quite calm about it in the car with Clive, but inside I was so excited I could almost hear my innards squeaking.

I haven't been to the theatre in London since Will took me on my special eleventh birthday. Only it was actually two months and five days after my REAL birthday, and in any case I was twelve, not eleven. (Red herrings? Mr Woods might say so.) But it was a very special time for Will and me. It's when I became Ariel Dee and stopped being Jessie Pike. And now Pat wants me to stop being Ariel and become Jecca. Would I be Jecca Dee or Jecca Pike, I wonder. Oh it's all so very confusing.

I notice I'm not writing this to Will. I don't know if I know why not or if I just don't want to acknowledge it...

•

'Have you done all your Christmas shopping, Jecca?' It was too cold to sit outside so these days they sat inside the cafeteria after class, drinking hot chocolate.

'Gosh no. Hardly any of it. Have you?' Christmas seemed to have crept up without warning – which couldn't really be true, given the multitude of flashy decorations all over Hexham.

'We could go into Newcastle on Saturday if you like. Have you got any money?'

'A bit.' She actually had most of her babysitting money, so the prospect of a day's shopping in Newcastle – and with Pat – had great appeal. 'I'll need to be back by about six though, for my babysitting job.'

'Are you still doing that? You're a trouper. I'll have a scrounge round and see what I can dig up in the way of disposable cash. Shall we get up madly early and take the nine o'clock train in?'

'We can try. Meantime let's get super-organised and make lists of who we need to buy for and what we might get them.'

'I already know who: Glyn, my mum and dad, and you. I can't afford anybody else.'

Ariel glowed inside. Pat was getting her a present! She was on an exclusive list with Pat's mother and father, and Glyn. Crikey! 'My list's a bit longer. I'd like to get the Parkers something – maybe something for Joy and Clive as well as something for each of the boys. Then there's the parents, maybe my mother – I don't know about her yet – my little brother perhaps, you of course, quite possibly Patrick, and perhaps even my tutor Paul. Though what on earth I could get him…'

'You have a brother? Blimey Ariel – I mean Jecca – what else are you keeping quiet about? And did I know you had a tutor? What's he like?'

'He's really old and a tiny bit stuffy, but he's been okay to me, so I'd quite like to give him something. Though as I say, I have no idea what…'

'Well that's the point of going Christmas shopping you ninny. If we knew what to get people we'd do it online. We can have fun shopping for him – we'll look in the sex shops for a start. Perhaps some skimpy underpants, thongs maybe, with a big red throbbing heart on them, strategically placed.'

'Pat!'

'Just kidding…. But wait a minute, what about your brother? Where is he? What's his name?'

'David. And he's in care at the moment. My mother isn't fit to take care of her children apparently. There was talk of him coming to live with the parents – Howard's his father too – but something went wrong when he came for a trial visit – he stole some money and got into a fight – and I think it's not going to happen now. And you know what? I'm not sorry. I didn't really like him when he was here. He's gone like our stepfather – who was the main reason I ran away from home in the first place.'

'Do you actually call your father Howard?'

'I don't usually call him anything to his face, but I do refer to him as Howard. I can't call him dad because Will was Dad to me for so long – even though I didn't actually call him that to his face either – he wouldn't have liked it.'

'I'll never get bored with you Ariel. I can't wait for Saturday so you can tell me more. Oops, bus coming….bye.'

•

'Mrs Parker rang up today, Jessie, and spoke to your father. Apparently you're invited to go to London with them in January. I think it's your Christmas present from them, which is very generous, I must say.' Ellen shook her head, smiling.

'I'll say! How lovely of them – may I go?'

'We – your father and I – don't see why not. They seem responsible people and I think an outing like that will do you the world of good.' Ellen looked as pleased for her as Ariel felt inside. 'But ask your father for the details – he just mentioned it briefly before he left for work.'

'Okay. I want to get a present for them, too – Pat and I are going Christmas shopping tomorrow. What sort of thing do you think I should be looking for? I thought I'd get a joint something for Clive and Joy and then two separate things for the little boys, maybe a book each.'

She and Ellen spent a pleasant thirty minutes discussing possibilities over a pot of tea with Ellen reluctant – Ariel could tell – to make any concrete suggestions about presents in case she said the wrong thing. Ariel felt sad about that. It wasn't Ellen's fault that Ariel hadn't really wanted to come and live with them. She decided that whatever she bought for Howard, she would buy something special for Ellen, just for her. Pat would know what to suggest.

TWELVE

Saturday

Taking a risk and writing my journal at the Parkers. (I actually came early so I could see the boys for a bit before they went to bed. Me! Imagine!) Normally the journal doesn't see the light of day outside my bedroom, and then mostly locked in my desk. Not that I really think that Patrick – if he even comes round tonight! – would read it without being invited. And he's not going to be invited. Ever. I wouldn't even show Pat most of it.

Will used to demand to read it. He said that the Durants always read what each other had written and either corrected or endorsed it. I don't think I wondered at the time how somebody can correct what you write in a journal since it's supposed to be about your feelings. I wonder about that now though. But I can't remember Will ever actually correcting anything. He didn't always read it, either, especially not towards the end when I deliberately kept it out of sight and he was too busy worrying about somebody finding out that he'd abducted me. And whatever other thing or things he felt guilty about.

(I can't believe I just wrote that. So casually, like it was nothing at all, when in fact it was the end of my life as I knew it.)

Christmas shopping today in Newcastle with Pat was the most fun I've had for years. In fact, I can't remember ever having fun quite like that. I certainly had a lot of fun with Will, but it was different. This was GIRL fun.

We managed the nine o'clock train – somewhat to our surprise, both of us. (And helped by it being five minutes late.) When we got there Pat said we'd earned a treat so we had morning coffee in a posh hotel. I think that was the last time all day we behaved anything like grown ups. Lunch was free samples from the food hall at some big department store and 'afternoon tea' was a three-scooper Baskin-Robbins ice cream: double chocolate ripple, bubble gum and pineapple sherbet for

Pat (she's working her way through all thirty-something flavours, she says). Boring vanilla, English toffee and Cornish clotted cream for me. I need to be more adventurous. I'm still stuffed, and glad Joy doesn't leave me a tray any longer but trusts me to help myself to whatever I want. At the moment that's nothing!

I'm very pleased with the presents I bought and crossed nearly everybody off my list. A book on the history of tractors (ALL boys of all ages love tractors, says Pat) for David; some make-up (of a tasteful variety) for my mother; two books of the right age for Graham and Nigel; some handkerchiefs (so he'll perhaps stop sniffing so much – it's beginning to get on my nerves)) for Howard and some ultra-luxurious bath salts (most expensive thing I bought; Pat was gobsmacked!) for Ellen. I may still buy something for the parents together, and I still need something for Joy and Clive. We had a lot of fun at Paul's expense, looking at highly inappropriate things for him. (I don't feel guilty yet, but I think I will later.) In the end I bought him a rather handsome leather case for his pens and pencil and things – of which he has many and can never seem to find the one he wants. I didn't buy anything for Pat – because she was with me, but I got some ideas* – and I didn't buy anything for Patrick, for whom I have NO idea. I think I'll probably end up not buying him anything. I don't really know him well enough. Pat did have a good suggestion though (to go with her many outrageous ones that caused her a lot of mirth and me lots of embarrassment): bake him something. I might do that. I make a rather good shortbread that most people really like. Then I would take it with me to babysitting on the Saturday before Christmas and see how I feel if and when he comes round.

I spent less than I'd mentally allowed myself. Which is good; I'm saving for the London trip now. Oh, I never told Pat about that.

* Ideas for Pat: The fluorescent socks she admired (which colour?); a CD or DVD token (horribly impersonal); a special journal or notebook (it has to be VERY special though – and would she ever use it?); some outrageous underwear (I wouldn't dare); a book of cartoons (safe); a set of 'artist's' pencils (though actually she seems happy enough with her felt tip pens for colouring round Glyn's name). Whatever it is, I must have it

wrapped and ready to take to her next week because Wednesday is our last class before the Christmas break. Oh dear, I'm going to miss that so much.

•

Christmas was a let-down. The Parkers hadn't needed her on the Saturday before the actual day, so she hadn't had to make a decision about the shortbread she'd finally, after much agonising, planned to make for Patrick, maybe to give to him. She was surprised at how disappointed she'd felt, but had gamely posted the books for Graham and Nigel with the gourmet cooking calendar for Clive and Joy. She had wanted to find a way to tell Joy that she was a little like Nigella Lawson herself so was sorry not to be able to see her and Clive open their present. Or the little boys, for that matter. Though she had been somewhat soothed by a lovely phone call from Joy on Boxing Day, saying all the right things about the presents and confirming that their present to her was the day trip to London.

Even worse was her disappointment at her present from Pat: a diary with an unrealistic-looking horse on the cover and a (cheap-looking) padlock. She couldn't help thinking it was a recycled gift; something Pat had received from someone else and, not being a diary-keeper herself, had simply passed it on. She chided herself for the less-than-gracious thought. Pat knew she kept a journal, so why wouldn't she have given her one for the coming year. Even so… Her gift to Pat – a stroke of absolute genius, she'd thought, had been a certificate to have her nails done at a flashy establishment in Hexham. And to be fair, Pat had been nothing but highly enthusiastic and appreciative about it, even suggesting that they share the token and have their nails done together. But while Ariel appreciated the thought and the girl-bonding gesture, she didn't really want her nails decorated with the sort of things Pat liked on hers. She actually didn't want her nails varnished at all.

There had been nothing – not even a card – from her mother or David. And of course nothing from Paul; she hadn't expected anything. He had been obviously greatly surprised and touched by her gift and had spent most of their last pre-Christmas lesson together loading his pens and pencils into the leather case, exclaiming with obvious pleasure as he did so.

Ellen had been gratifyingly happy with her bath salts, too: 'How did you know that this is my favourite scent?', and Howard had professed mild but apparently genuine pleasure and some amusement at his handkerchiefs. Their gift to Ariel had been a generous cheque and a box of assorted toffees from Thorntons. She tried hard not to acknowledge the tinge of disappointment she felt. After all, they still didn't really know her. Even though she'd been with them for almost two years. But in any case, what could they have given her that wouldn't have been a disappointment? And it was a very generous cheque.

Ellen had gone to quite some trouble to make what she kept calling 'a proper Christmas dinner', so Ariel had tried to join in with her enthusiasm; wearing the stupid paper hat and laughing hollowly at the equally stupid jokes from the crackers. They'd watched some boring television together and then, claiming a headache about nine o'clock, Ariel had gone up to her room to compare last year's list of carols heard with this year's. In the deep midwinter topped both lists, having been played in her hearing 11 times last year and 17 this season. She wondered how she could make the listing more interesting. Perhaps she should note where she had heard each carol? She'd think about it for next year; there wouldn't be any more carols after today. Which wasn't a bad thing. She'd heard enough.

She lay on her bed, trying not to think of what Christmas had been like with Will and what it probably was like, today, at the Parkers. Would Patrick be there? Had the children liked the books she'd chosen for them? And would Joy be pleased with the calendar? She wondered how Pat's day had gone. She couldn't imagine Pat having a boring day. What had the Durants done on Christmas Days, when they were alive? 'I'll bet they had a better time than this,' she thought miserably, and got up to count, on the calendar, how many days before the Philosophy and Logic class resumed. Fourteen. Thirteen, if you counted today as gone, which she might as well. She drew a black line through 25th December on the calendar and focused on what she might do to get through the remaining thirteen days.

THIRTEEN

Saturday

P&L starts again on Tuesday, and babysitting starts again tonight! I can hardly wait. My life seems to have been on hold since mid-December. I haven't even seen Pat, though we have talked on the phone a couple of times. Her Christmas was good, she said; she spent the whole day with Glyn and didn't have to sit through a pretend-jolly lunch with her parents. She was pretty vague about where they went and what they did, but I gather there was a lot of kissing and 'you know...'. Actually, I don't know, but I wasn't going to risk her scorn by saying so.

Paul thinks I should take another class at the college. I like that thought, but have no idea what to choose. He says I won't have much of a selection because not much starts in the January term, but on Monday we are going to look at what my options are. Turns out he actually knows Mr Woods and says he (P) will phone him to see what he (Mr W) might suggest.

So what with all that and the proposed day out in London, life is looking up. I'm looking forward to being happy again. I don't think I'm cut out to be sad.

•

'Patrick says you're interested in cricket, Ariel, and that you might want to come to the local matches next summer. Clive plays in the same team – along with a friend of ours, Eric – and they've asked me if I'll help out with the teas again next summer. I said I'd think about it, but I'd do it in a heartbeat if you'd do it with me – then one of us could slice up tomatoes and cucumbers and things while the other watches Graham and Nigel to make sure they don't get themselves in front of the sight screen or run off with the ball. They clearly love you to bits and you don't seem entirely indifferent to them, I must say.' Joy beamed at her.

'I'd love to help.' Ariel had no hesitation. 'Just let me know when.'

'Middle of April is the start. Weather permitting of course. And speaking of dates, we've decided on a fortnight today for the London jaunt. Okay with you?'

'Of course. I'm really looking forward to it. Are the boys coming too?'

'Oh no, they wouldn't enjoy it. And neither should we if we had to deal with them all day. No-no, Clive will stay home and look after them.'

'Clive? I thought he was coming too.' Ariel was confused.

'No, but don't worry, we won't be by ourselves. Patrick is coming, and our friend Eric. They'll take turns with the driving and we'll sit in the back and criticise.'

Ariel opened her mouth to ask if the parents knew exactly who was going and who wasn't, and then shut it again. What difference could it make? It made a huge difference to her, of course, that Patrick was coming; she couldn't really care less about Eric instead of Clive. If she brought it up with the parents they might feel they had to get the whole thing sanctioned by The Team. She definitely didn't want that.

What on earth would she wear? She'd have to get Pat's advice on that, though of course she'd need to tone down to her own comfort level whatever Pat suggested. They hadn't exactly fallen out over their differing choice of wardrobes and styles, but they had, at times, come close. On second thoughts, maybe she wouldn't involve Pat. Ellen would actually be a better bet; she seemed to understand and accept Ariel's dress code, such as it was.

She suddenly remembered something. 'What was your maiden name, Joy?'

'My maiden name? Cavendish. But why on earth do you want to know that? Oh I know...you're trying to find out Patrick's last name without asking. Very sly, Ariel, very sly. Oh heavens, I've made you blush again. I'm sorry. Are you a tiny bit keen on my little brother?'

Ariel didn't know where to look or what to say. Fortunately Joy either recognised that or realised she was late for meeting Clive – or both. She swept up her handbag and scarf, shrugged herself into her coat and left with a cheery, 'Have a good evening – Patrick's probably coming round.'

Cavendish. Patrick Cavendish. Ariel Cavendish. Jecca Cavendish? She sat at the table and opened her notebook. NO! She would NOT write Patrick and Ariel Cavendish and draw flowers around it. What if Patrick – if he came – opened her notebook and saw that? She felt herself blushing again and fled to the bathroom to see how awful she looked.

She splashed cold water on her face and finger-combed her hair into a neater shape. Deep breath. If Patrick turned up, what might they talk about tonight? London? The cricket matches next summer? Oh, no, she could ask his advice on what other courses she might take at the college. That felt much safer – there was something about recognising his greater knowledge that felt rather comforting and evoked a memory of just such times between her and Will. He had been a great teacher and she had relished being his student.

FOURTEEN

Sunday

One of the best things about Patrick is how easy he is to be with. Quite like Will, actually. He was lovely about my prospective enhanced college career and said he thought I ought to see if I could get onto the advanced course of P&L – though he thought it would be either one or the other (P or L) at that level, not both. He said he didn't see why I couldn't manage both of them, as well as the one I'm taking. And he kept saying it would be up to me, that I mustn't listen only to what other people want for me. I said Paul and Mr Woods would doubtless have a huge say in what I do or don't do and he asked me how I felt about that. I said I didn't know (which is true -- I was too busy trying to act reasonably grown up!) but thinking about it later I realise I trust both of them. And, oddly, I trust Patrick too. Maybe because he does keep stressing how important it is for me to have the main say in what I do. There aren't many in my life who do that at the moment.

But the advanced course! That would be wonderful; I know I'd love it. And if I had to choose only one of them I think I'd plump for logic. I do like philosophy a lot, but the challenge of logic is still quite thrilling to me and it's the part of the P&L course I enjoy the most. It gives me lovely happy memories of my time with Will.

Of course I'd have to continue with the P&L course I'm on now – otherwise I'd NEVER keep up with an advanced one! Besides, I don't want to lose touch with Pat. I don't think I would, but there's something reassuring about knowing I'll see her anyway every Tuesday, Wednesday and Friday.

Interesting how she lives next door to the Parkers yet I never see her when I'm there on Saturdays. She's probably out, like most of the rest of the world! Her with Glyn, Joy with Clive, Ellen and Howard sometimes ... and there's me and Patrick like an old married couple, drinking tea while the boys sleep the sleep of the innocent upstairs.

Crikey! Until I just wrote that, I'd COMPLETELY forgotten that he'd actually said something like that last night. I don't think he used the 'm' word, but he did comment on what a cosy domestic scene it was, him and me with tea (for me, cider for him), sitting by the Parkers' fire with the children asleep upstairs.

I think he must like me a little bit. He said he was looking forward to the London outing, but didn't mention the cricket again. Perhaps that's too far away. And anyway who knows what water will have gone under our respective bridges by next summer.

●

For probably the first time in their history, she was excited about seeing Paul on Monday. She hoped he'd had the chance to talk to Mr Woods so possibly she could get started on her new class immediately.

He didn't disappoint. 'Mr Woods was very complimentary about you, Jessica. That is, once he realised who we were talking about – he says he calls you Ariel because you asked him to. I didn't know that.'

'Oh sorry, Paul. I used to ask people to call me Ariel but nobody ever would, so I suppose when I met you I'd given up asking.'

'But you asked Mr Woods?'

'Yes. I think I thought in a totally new environment...' she trailed off, not quite knowing how else to explain it. 'Anyway, what did he say? Can I go to extra classes?'

'You may. And you can. As I said, he was very pleased with you and feels you have a fine mind and that you have great potential. As do I. It's simply a question of what would be your best option. I explained to him about your home-schooling and he agreed with me that we need to keep an eye on the requirements now for you to get into university eventually.'

'University? Crikey!' Wait till I tell Patrick that, she thought. And Pat.

'As I have said, we are limited at the moment by what is available. I have a list….ah, yes, here it is. I think we can safely ignore Woodworking and Auto-mechanics…so we have Conversational French, English literature, Geology and Ethics. Unless you are passionately interested in old rock formations, I'd suggest the French or English Lit. The Ethics course is probably very similar to what you are currently taking.'

'Is it a sort of next-level up though? If it is, I think I'd like that a lot. I don't fancy French at all, I'm afraid.'

'Then what about English Lit? He did tell me what they are reading but I'm afraid it hasn't stayed with me. At my age they all begin to sound the same, though of course they are not.'

Ariel closed her eyes and struggled to recall Patrick's earnest urging her not to be overwhelmed by what somebody else wanted for her. She suddenly

remembered C S Lewis's subject.

'There isn't a Medieval Literature course, I suppose?'

Paul shook his head sorrowfully, so she took a deep breath and tried again. 'I still think I'd like the Ethics course though, especially if it's an advanced version of the one I'm taking now. Which I'd carry on with, of course.'

'Well. Interestingly Mr Woods actually said he sees a career for you along that path and he therefore would urge you to opt for Ethics. Myself, being a dyed-in-the-wool – if not stick-in-the-mud – Lit-man,' he smiled his lop-sided smile, 'I'd see more of a future for you down that road. But…essentially it's up to you. They are both what the college calls 'short courses' running for about eight weeks, I believe, and both begin early in February. I'd suggest you sleep on it and possibly talk to Mr Woods yourself tomorrow.'

'I will, yes I will. Thank you.' Ariel hoped she wouldn't have to concentrate on anything too challenging with Paul this morning. Her mind was leaping ahead to what she would say to

Mr Woods. And what she would say to Pat – could Pat do the extra courses with her? She suddenly realised she had no idea what Pat did with the rest of her life – apart from being with Glyn, of course.

'Do you wish me to call you Ariel from now on? I'm happy to do that, if I can remember.' Paul looked at her over his minuscule reading glasses, perched precariously on the end of his rather long nose, waiting for her answer.

'Oh. I don't know. No, I don't think I do actually. I think I'm Jessica to you.' Ariel didn't know which shocked her more: Paul's question or her own response.

•

'What were you and the Woodsman cooking up when I came in?' Pat had been slightly late this morning, so Ariel had taken the opportunity to mention her conversation with Paul to Mr Woods.

'He thinks I'm good enough to take the eight-week Ethics course if I want to.' She tried to sound casual.

'And do you? Personally I can't think of anything more deadly than a continuation of this lot.'

'Actually I do. And if you ask me, you're good enough to do it, too – if you wanted to. I wish you would. It's far more fun with you than it would be by myself.'

Pat exaggerated her look of surprise. 'No kidding. Let's face it, life with me is always going to be more fun than going solo. But no thanks. What little time I have left over from keeping Glyn happy so he won't go looking at other females is, alas, taken up by flipping sixth-form obligations. Some of us go to school you know.'

'Oh, no, I didn't know. Sorry. I haven't been to school since I was eleven, so being in a class with other people is quite exciting for me. Especially when you're in it.'

'You'll find somebody to keep you in the real world. Won't

be as exciting as me though. You can count on that.'

'I know.' She felt sad. 'You'll always be my best friend though.'

'Oh god, don't go all maudlin on me.' But Pat was pleased, Ariel could tell.

FIFTEEN

Saturday – 6:20 AM

London Day! Clive is picking me up at seven o'clock and taking me to their house where presumably Patrick and the other friend will join us. We're to set off from there as soon as we are assembled. I'm ready now – been up since half-past five.

I think I look quite nice. After trying on four or five different 'ensembles' as Ellen calls them, I've settled on my brown tweedy skirt, and an orange and brown and blue jumper with a new crisp white shirt underneath. Ellen says her mother said you should always wear white next to your face and in this case I think she's probably right. It sets off the whole outfit really nicely. My hair looks pretty good – I had it cut last week and it's at its best today. Nice brown, tiny-cabled tights and my comfortable shoes that actually have a bit of a heel. I'm pretty sure Pat would not entirely approve, but somewhat to my surprise I don't think I mind. It's important for me to be comfortable and I am. As well as feeling I look pretty good. 'An unbeatable combination,' Ellen said. She's been great over all this. She's even lent me her sheepskin coat that sets off the whole thing just right. And offered, but didn't push, some make up, but I'm not going that far.

And I haven't thought much if at all about what Will would make of this. It all seems so far removed from my life with him.

Wonder what I'll be writing in here next Saturday.

•

'My you look nice!' Joy was still in her dressing gown, hurriedly buttering toast for Graham and trying to pour milk for Nigel. 'I know it doesn't look like it, but I'll be ready in ten minutes.'

'Here, let me help.' Ariel finished buttering the toast, cut it into strips, and put it in front of Graham at the same time as she put down the cup of milk for Nigel. 'What else should they have?'

'Anything they want. Just keep them quiet so we can leave without Clive regretting his offer. I'm off to get dressed. Oh, that'll be Eric or Patrick, or maybe even both…' she disappeared upstairs as Ariel began scrambling eggs for the little boys, and Clive apparently went to answer the doorbell.

'Ariel, hello!' Patrick appeared in the kitchen, 'This is my friend and opening partner Eric Pearson. Eric – Ariel.'

He was older than Patrick by the look of it, perhaps about Joy and Clive's age, with sandy hair and huge bushy eyebrows to match, and definitely on the plump side. He had a nice smile. 'Pleased to meet you, Ariel. I've heard a lot about you.'

She smiled back at him. 'Hello. Hello Patrick, too.' She hadn't given too much thought to what Eric would be like, but even so was pleased that she already felt comfortable with him. He looked, she thought, like a much-loved and slightly dishevelled teddy bear. Unlike Patrick, who looked – what? sleek? Was that the right word for him? In a good way though.

Joy wasn't exaggerating by much when she'd said ten minutes, and they were actually on the M1 heading south before nine o'clock. Patrick said he'd take the first driving shift. Eric sat beside him in front, Joy sat behind Patrick and Ariel sat behind Eric, whose bulk made it hard for her to see anything other than Patrick's profile in the rear view mirror. Stupidly, she hadn't realised he could see her watching him – until he winked at her. Embarrassed, she turned her head and vowed she'd only look out of the side window from now on. Knowing he could still see her, she struggled to keep herself from frowning as she scolded herself for being 'so infantile'. She hoped she hadn't blushed.

It was a long drive. They stopped at Tibshelf Services for petrol and take-away hamburgers and chips, as well as (for Ariel at least) a much-needed bathroom break. She tried to pay her share for the food but Joy said 'No, this is all part of your much-deserved Christmas present.' Eric drove instead of Patrick, who was now in front of Ariel and she felt she could relax a little as she contemplated the back of his rather shapely head and neck. She and Pat had talked a lot about the importance of the back of men's necks, ears, backs-of-hands, and teeth, and she thought with pleasure that she could tell Pat that Patrick was ten out of ten on all fronts – or in this case, she stifled a giggle – backs. She'd have to be careful how she phrased it though; Glyn was apparently nowhere near a ten for the teeth, having been in a fight in prison, Pat had said, and lost a couple. She didn't want Pat to feel bad for her man.

Thinking about the most tactful way to pass on the information she wanted to about Patrick served a useful function. It kept her from dwelling on what she wasn't sure she had really seen as they'd walked back to car. She had been deep in conversation with Patrick about the absurdity of how wonderful hamburgers could taste when you were in a good mood, a holiday mood, when in reality you knew they tasted like ground chipboard. Joy and Eric were walking behind them and when she had turned around to make sure they were all together, they had seemed to be holding hands. She'd looked away immediately. She must have been mistaken. Or else it was just exuberance on their part at the prospect of a day out. Yes, that's what it must have been.

'What are we going to see, Joy?' It suddenly dawned on Ariel that she had no idea – though it absolutely didn't matter; she was up for anything.

'Don't know yet. What we'll do is park the car in Tesco's at Swiss Cottage and take the tube into central London. Then we'll visit my father who is deputy manager of a tickets outlet. He will almost certainly be able to get us some last minute tickets for free, but we might not have much of a choice. Do you have any preferences, Ariel?

'Gosh, no. I was just thinking, I'm happy to see anything. In any case, I don't even know what's on.' She didn't want to say so, but she hoped it wouldn't be The Mikado – or indeed any Gilbert and Sullivan – as that would be a too-poignant reminder of her time in London with Will. What a little girl she'd been then. Mad about the escalators in the Underground, and struggling to be as grown-up as she could for Will because she'd known without realising she'd known it that that was what he wanted. Crikey! Second uncomfortable thought of the day: first the Joy and Eric holding-hands thing and now – though not for the first time – more awareness of how Will's need for her to be a certain way had so often clashed with her own need for an all-nurturing, all-loving father, as well as the great teacher that he undoubtedly was. 'Bloody hell,' she thought, unconsciously borrowing Pat's language, 'I was only flipping twelve!'

•

Joy's father gave them 'best seats in the house' for a play none of them had ever heard of. Ariel found it incomprehensible and anxiously watched the others to see if she could pick up any clues on how to react. Patrick, next to her, was watching it all very solemnly, but with a frown; Joy and Eric on the other side of him, kept giggling and whispering to each other and seemed to be enjoying themselves. The theatre was less than half full, which, Patrick said – somewhat to Ariel's relief – was hardly surprising. 'What a load of utter crap,' he added, as they filed out into the late afternoon twilight.

'Oh, it wasn't that bad…' Joy said.

'Yes it was,' Eric said firmly. 'But who cares? Let's have a drink and a decent dinner to fuel us for the return journey. Yes?'

They walked past several souvenir shops that Ariel would loved to have looked in, but didn't feel able to say so. She badly wanted to buy something as a memento of her day out. She also wanted to get something for Pat and possibly Ellen, neither of whom had ever been to London, she'd discovered. She hadn't known what to expect from the day out in London, but she hoped this wasn't all there was to it.

'Do you want to do any shopping, Ariel?' Joy took her arm. 'We're not too far from Harrods, I think – let's go there and have a prowl round. And you men folk can relax in the bar upstairs if you'd rather.'

To Ariel's relief and joy, there was agreement all round. She and Joy left the men admiring the sumptuous displays in the

Food Hall and, having promised to meet them in the bar in about an hour, set off to explore. Ariel had never seen anything like it. The hour went by much too quickly, but she did find a scarf she felt sure Ellen would like and that went really well with the sheepskin jacket, and a pair of dazzling black and silver tights she knew would bowl Pat over.

'What are you getting for you?' Joy had several green Harrods bags hanging from her wrist. 'I'm embarrassed to say that almost all of this is for me. Even the shirts for the boys are really for me because I love the embroidered frogs and I want to see my sons wearing them.'

'Shouldn't we be going back to Patrick and Eric?'

'They can wait. They'll be happy enough in the bar – even if it's non-alcoholic beer and anyway, how often do we have a chance to shop in Harrods? Come on, let's find a top or something for you.' She grabbed Ariel's arm and steered her into the appropriate department, where they found a pale brown silk blouse that Ariel knew she absolutely had to have. Joy was enthusiastically admiring, which made it an entirely satisfactory purchase. She even dared think that Pat would approve.

In the lift to the top floor Joy put her hand on Ariel's arm. 'Ariel, I probably don't have to say this, but anything you see with Eric and me....well, I know you won't say anything to anybody.'

Ariel didn't know how to respond, so as was her custom under such circumstances, said nothing. She stared hard at the lift door and hoped Joy wouldn't say anything else.

'I'd never do anything to hurt Clive. You know that. It's all a bit of harmless fun, but I can see how it might look like something it isn't. Okay?'

Ariel nodded. She wondered how she could change the subject. She just wouldn't look at Eric and Joy, then she wouldn't have to see anything she didn't want to see.

SIXTEEN

Sunday

Why is it that whenever I write in my journal I'm an absolute mess of conflicted feelings? Yesterday, the trip to London, was fabulous in so many ways, but utterly awful in another. I don't know what to make of Joy and Eric. I know what she said – 'it's all a bit of harmless fun' – but I don't like it. She's married to Clive and he obviously adores her. And I thought she adored him. Well, she does. But can you 'adore' two people at once in the way she seems to? Or is she lying about her feelings about either Eric or Clive. And if so, which one? And is it any of my business anyway?

Crikey I'm tired today. I thought we'd never leave London last night. Dinner dragged on and on and then we still had nearly six hours of driving. I liked being in the front with Patrick when he drove, chatting about this and that, even though it was hard to ignore what was happening in the back seat. I was also nervous that when Eric drove, he'd want Joy in front with him and I'd be in the back with Patrick and he might want us to do what E & J were doing. Fortunately Joy was asleep when the drivers changed places, so I just moved into the back with her, and Patrick stayed in front with Eric, 'to navigate', he said.

I didn't want to stay the night – what was left of it – at Joy's, but was frankly too exhausted to argue. Clive was already in bed and asleep when we got there, so Joy gave me a blanket and a pillow and I collapsed on their sofa in a pair of Clive's (much too big) pyjamas. I was ages falling asleep and then dreamed I'd got separated from Joy in Harrods and couldn't find her or the bar where Eric and Patrick would be. None of it looked familiar, not that I know the place at all anyway, but I couldn't find anywhere I recognised and kept going down dead end corridors. Oh, I couldn't find my new blouse either. I seemed to have put it down somewhere but couldn't remember. I wondered how I could describe it to Pat well enough for her to know it was a stunner.

Nice when I woke up this morning though, and the little boys discovered me on the sofa. 'Air-rull! Air-rull!' Nigel kept exclaiming in obvious delight, and they both got under the blanket with me for a cuddle. 'Why are you wearing my Daddy's jammies?' Graham wanted to know. Clive made us all waffles for breakfast and then brought me home about half past eleven.

Ellen is very pleased with her scarf but when she nearly began crying I felt very uncomfortable. Fortunately she saw that and made herself stop right away. Then I felt bad that I hadn't even thought about buying anything for Howard. Can't wait till Tuesday to give Pat her tights and tell her I found out that Patrick is a solicitor, 'articled' to his uncle's firm, whatever that means.

•

Pat was exultant. 'You bought these for me! From Harrods! You absolute dreamboat! I don't know what I love more: that you bought them for me on your romantic junket in London – from Harrods no less – or that you actually got me something I love. You're coming on very nicely Jecca-Ariel Dee-Pike, aka my best friend.'

Ariel was equally happy. She'd never had a best friend, unless you could count Will and that hadn't been the same thing at all. She floated – on air, she felt – into class with Pat.

'Right, who has the provocative quote for me today? Alan! I don't often hear from you – what have you unearthed for our delectation and critique?' Mr Woods waited expectantly but patiently as the boy sitting in front of Pat shuffled through his notes and adjusted his glasses on his nose.

'C S Lewis: Friendship is born at that moment when one person says to another "what! You too? I thought I was the only one".'

'Hm, not bad. Thank you Alan. What do you think group? Pat?'

Ariel was surprised to see her friend's hand go straight up. Pat didn't usually contribute much to class discussions though she was obviously a deeper thinker than she seemed, as she always got good marks for her assignments.

'I don't think it's NOT true, but I don't think that's the only way friendship is born. Not my friendships, anyway.'

'He didn't say that, Pat,' A girl whose name Ariel didn't know spoke up. 'He didn't say "the only way friendship is formed".'

'Well he didn't say "one way a friendship is formed" either,' Pat retorted.

Mr Woods banged the flat of his hand on the table. 'Red herrings, red herrings. Haven't you learned anything, you thick-as-two-planks morons?'

The debate continued, monitored by Mr Woods, who broke in from time to time to point out the fallacy of a particular argument or his personal bête noir: red herrings. Ariel desperately wanted unilateral and unstinting praise for her erstwhile hero, but at the same time was really pleased at Pat's adamant defence of their friendship that had not begun that way. 'How odd that friendship is the topic today when I was just thinking how lucky I am to have you as my friend,' she whispered to Pat.

'Trick question, trick question; I keep telling you, they're all trick questions,' Pat hissed back.

At the end of the class Mr Woods gestured to Ariel to wait and, when the rest of the class had disappeared said, 'I'm delighted you have signed up for the Ethics course Ariel. I see great things ahead for you and I want to do my part to ensure you don't fritter away that fine brain of yours on things like cinéma vérité and underwater basket-weaving. Between us, Paul Greenbow and I, we'll get you into a first-class university for a first-class honours degree as starters. Yes?' He thrust his head forward and glared at her.

Ariel was not deceived by his fierceness and smiled. 'Thank you. It's taken me a bit by surprise, but I do like the idea, so I appreciate your advice. Paul's too.'

'Good. See you tomorrow. Dismissed!'

•

She hurried out, happy to see that Pat had waited. She was longing to tell Pat about the London day out although had still not made up her mind just how much she could tell.

But first of course Pat wanted to know why she'd been asked to wait. Ariel started to tell her but suddenly realised that Pat might feel left out or overlooked or in some way diminished. 'I'm sure he'd feel the same about you...' she trailed off.

'He'd be wasting his time. No uni for yours truly. I'm killing myself getting top marks with this lot – there's no brain power left for more.'

'What do you want to do then, when you leave school?'

'What I do now, only for more hours. Fettle Glyn's office work and be his attractive receptionist and sit-on-his-knee-for-dictation secretary for his soon-to-be massively successful building company.'

'I didn't know that, Pat. I didn't know you already worked for anybody, let alone for Glyn.' Ariel didn't like how she felt at not having known this side of Pat's life. Should she somehow have known? Should she have asked more questions? Had Pat told her and she hadn't taken it in?

'Well you wouldn't know. I haven't said anything. Don't be in such a hurry to beat yourself up. It's nothing but masochistic and extremely unattractive. And I haven't said anything because it's only a couple of hours a month at the moment. Not to mention that he doesn't actually have a company yet, but that's the plan. They taught him bricklaying and plastering in prison, so he thinks he's well ready. But anyway, that's boring. And frankly, so is your proposed university career. I want to know about last Saturday. Everything please.'

They settled themselves in the corner of the cafeteria with a hot chocolate each. 'Well, to start with he's a trainee solicitor and his last name is Cavendish.' Ariel proudly revealed these items. She forgave herself for letting Pat believe she'd only just learned his name, because she didn't want to own up to the now obviously idiotic way she had gone about finding out.

'Cavendish, eh? Not a bad name for a solicitor though. And posh, but not too posh, like Arrowby-Blackstone. That's way over the top, if you ask me.'

'Arrowby who? I thought his name was Alan.'

'It is. It's Alan Arrowby-Blackstone. He's in my sixth-form class and a bit of a drip as well. Anyway, red herring, red herring, as Teach would say. Back to your Patrick. Jecca Cavendish has rather a nice ring to it if you ask me. What did you wear?'

Ariel did her best to look and sound nonchalant. 'Oh, a brown skirt and an orange top, nothing outrageous.'

'Why ever not? You should have worn some come-hither stuff, cleavage-enhancing and so on. I would. But then I've never aspired to the twinset and pearls brigade. I suppose your stepmother approved?'

'She did, as a matter of fact, but then she seems to understand that it's more important to me to feel comfortable with what I'm wearing.'

'Ouch! Okay, okay, I take your point.' Pat reached over and patted Ariel's arm. 'Olive branch offered.' She put her head on one side and smiled beguilingly. 'Olive branch accepted?'

Ariel nodded, unsure whether she was more hurt by the comment or touched by Pat's obvious and immediate remorse. 'I've a good mind now not to show you the stunning blouse I bought in Harrods.'

'You will. You need my admiring approval. And you've accepted the olive branch, don't forget. But onto more important details – did you two sit in the back of the car and get indiscreetly up close and personal?'

'No, he never sat in the back. I sat in the front with him for a while when he was driving on the way back though. That was nice. That's when I found out about his job.' (But not his name; she'd own up to Pat about that some other time.)

'What a crass waste of a back seat. The Parkers can get cuddly any time, they don't need a trip to London and the back seat of a car.'

'Actually Mr Parker didn't come. A friend of theirs came and he sat in the back with Mrs Parker.' Ariel saw her mistake too late.

'No kidding! I'll bet that was Eric somebody or other and I'll bet he and Mrs P got very up close and personal. Yes, they did, didn't they? I can tell by your face.'

Ariel was mortified. 'She asked me not to say anything to anybody,' she whispered.

'I'll bet she did! Well you didn't. I knew without you saying anything. Half our street knows about Eric Thingy and Mrs Parker anyway. I should think the only person who doesn't know is Mr Parker. And you of course.'

Ariel was stunned into silence. She stirred her chocolate drink repeatedly and became aware that she was shaking her head slowly from side to side in absolute disbelief. Pat reached over and patted her arm again. 'Are you shocked? Yes, I can see you are. I'm sorry – I thought you'd know. Don't let it spoil things for you.'

'How can Clive not know if everybody else does?'

'Well perhaps he does know but doesn't want to do anything about it. Maybe he's got a bit on the side as well, so this suits him just fine. I don't know. I don't understand men.' Pat drained her hot chocolate and got up to leave. 'And they probably prefer it that way. But I keep working on it.'

SEVENTEEN

Saturday

Dear Will,

You of all people will know how quickly life can change. I can't believe all that has happened since I wrote in here last Saturday. And yet really, nothing has changed. Only my perception of what is happening and goes on happening whether I know about it or not. (I feel Mr Woods' influence here, getting me to look at 'facts' quite critically. And funnily enough, it helps. It stops my stomach churning in the way that usually only counting things does. Sometimes I don't like feelings.)

My friend Pat seems totally unaffected by it all and isn't behaving any differently as far as I can see. But then, why should she? She's apparently known about 'the situation' (I can't bring myself to write any names) for ages and seems quite blasé about it. We've hardly talked about it since the bombshell dropped on Tuesday. And in fact, we haven't spent a great deal of time together after class because my new Ethics course started this week too.

Am I enjoying it? I am indeed. Well, I think I am. The instructor is very different from Mr Woods and his way of teaching is a lot drier and often hard to follow, but so far I think I'm keeping up. I'm taking copious notes and hoping that when we get the first assignment I'll have a sense of what to do. There isn't, as yet anyway, much class discussion, and I think I'm a bit relieved about that. I think my style is – or has become – 'watchful waiting' until I know where things are going and I feel safe to contribute.

Babysitting tonight. I'm not going early for a change. I don't want to spend any extra time with Joy at the moment.

Oh Will. I'm struggling so hard NOT to say 'I wish you were here'. I'm feeling horribly out of my depth and so in need of your commonsense attitude with all this. And yet, I've moved so far on from where I was with you that I'm not sure how even you could help at this point.

I'm not making any sense. Simply put, if you were here, I wouldn't be in this turmoil! Simple as.

I'm also aware of how much I seem to have assumed that you are 'looking down on me' and therefore know what on earth I'm writing about. And I know how much you'd dislike that idea. Oh dear, another example of how our wants and needs are moving wider and wider apart. (Or am I just now noticing that?)

If I were doing my journaling on the computer I'd probably delete all this.

•

'You're looking quite sad these days. Is everything all right?' She and Ellen were sitting over a second cup of coffee at breakfast. Howard was on weekend duty at the local hospital where he worked as a porter, so they felt free to linger. Especially as it was Sunday and neither of them had any obligations looming.

'I think so. Everything is all right in my little world, but I'm not sure about some other worlds. Maybe that's what makes me feel sad.' Ariel realised as she spoke the truth of what she had just said. 'Yes, I'm loving my life really. I shouldn't be sad.'

'But you are. If I can help, you are very welcome to talk to me, you know. I'm not that much older than you actually, so I can well remember what it felt like to be nearly sixteen. And as soon as I said that, I remembered how irritating it was when people said that to me!' She smiled at Ariel. 'But the offer stands. And unless you've robbed a bank, I shan't necessarily feel compelled to share anything you say with your father.'

'Thanks, Ellen. But at the moment I need to sort it out in my head so I can make some sense of what I'm unhappy about.'

'Boyfriend trouble? I've had plenty of experience on that

stage.'

'No, not at all. I don't really have a boy friend anyway. No, it's other people who are married yet don't always behave like it. With other people, if you know what I mean.'

Ellen sipped her coffee. 'I think I do. It's not easy to watch people behave in a way that instinctively you know isn't right, but not everybody lives their life by my rules, I have to remember that.'

'Can you still be friends with people who don't?'

'Can I? Or do you mean can you? Or even can one?'

'I don't really know, Ellen. And I don't know what to do.'

'Then I'd suggest that you don't do anything for now. Once you've actually done something there's often no going back, but if you take a wait-and-see attitude you can usually see, later, what the best or right thing to do is.'

Ariel nodded solemnly. 'Yes. That makes sense to me and actually is how I normally operate. I think I just needed somebody to remind me. So thank you, Ellen!'

She suddenly felt much better. She didn't have to do anything, and certainly not immediately. She realised with relief that she could go on behaving normally with Joy – she'd hated being 'distant' during the past couple of weeks. And as she'd written to Will via her journal, nothing had changed except her awareness of it. She would keep that in mind; it would help.

•

'Why was Glyn in prison, Pat?' She looked at her friend to see if she was offended at the question and thought she was not

'Fraud, technically. Some sort of dodgy deal with the people he was working for – selling their extra bits and not telling them. It wasn't really a big deal – he got three months and a hefty fine, which he'll be paying off for the rest of his life I imagine.

Why?'

'Just wondering. You seem so unruffled about it, so I thought it couldn't have been anything really nasty.'

'Nah. This sort of thing that goes on all the time – he was just unlucky and got rumbled. But actually I think it's taught him a lesson – he's determined to be all straight and above board now. "So you don't have to worry about me", he says. Sweet, eh?'

Ariel smiled and nodded. There was something really comfortable about Pat and Glyn's relationship that gave her genuine pleasure. Even when they'd had what Pat called a flaming row, there was an easy solidity, a permanence about it. Pat sometimes joked about 'keeping Glyn happy' but Ariel never got a sense that she – or Glyn, for that matter – was anything other than complacent – in an entirely good way – about the relationship.

'Speaking of being detained at Her Majesty's pleasure, what do you think your Will did that made the powers-that-be so interested?'

'Well he abducted me, for a start. That's all I know about. Wouldn't that be enough?'

'It could be, but I thought you'd said they were trying to pin something else on him. Aren't you curious about that?'

'No, I'm not.' Ariel could hear herself sounding frosty. 'I don't want to know. I'm sure whatever he did or didn't do was for a very good reason. I think he was a very honourable man, actually.'

'Well he can't be that honourable – he abducted you, leaving your parents to wonder if they'd ever see you alive again. I can't imagine how my parents would ever recover from something like that.'

'My parents – my mother and stepfather anyway – were, are, nothing like your parents. And you're beginning to sound like the social workers and counsellors. What people don't understand is that Will had a dream, a vision to make the world a better place for everybody, not just the top echelon. And I was his chosen helpmeet. I'm proud of that.' Ariel could feel herself getting upset. Why would Pat put her in this position, having to defend Will? Pat was her friend, for heaven's sake. 'Here's your bus anyway.'

'Okay, okay, don't get mad with me. YOU started this conversation about our respective blokes and their crimes and misdemeanours remember.'

Ariel didn't respond. She was angry with Pat and angry with herself for talking as much as she had about Will and her time with him. She vowed that would be the last time. And just see if Pat still wanted to be friends without the titillation of stories of Will and Ariel. Probably not. Probably her only appeal to Pat was what Pat saw as her sensational story. Damn, she wanted to cry, she mustn't. She turned away as Pat got on her bus, leaving her to trudge home, angry and unhappy.

•

'What was your bloke's name before he changed it to Will Whatever, Ariel?' Pat was behaving as if their contretemps the day before had not happened. She'd waited at the bus stop for Ariel's bus, as usual, and as usual they'd walked to class together. Ariel wasn't speaking, but Pat had not seemed to notice. Now, after class, they were slowly making their way back to the bus stop.

'I don't know. I asked him, but he said he'd forgotten.' She did her best to match Pat for casualness, ignoring her vow to never talk to Pat again about Will, and pleased that her friend was apparently willing to behave normally.

'Don't be daft. You can't forget your name.' Pat frowned. 'He just didn't want to tell you in case you looked him up on the internet and found out things he didn't want you to know.'

'I would never have done that!' Ariel was shocked. 'And he did forget. He taught himself to forget all sorts of things he didn't want to remember – like his real birthday, for example. He taught me to forget things, too. I've found that very useful as a matter of fact.'

'Like what?'

'I can't remember. Obviously.' She glared at Pat who started to laugh.

'Oh okay. I get the message. Shut up Pat and mind your own business. Okay. Got time for a hot choccy before your ethics class? I'll buy.'

Ariel recognised the gesture but wasn't quite ready. 'It's not ethics today,' she muttered, 'and I can buy my own drink, thank you.'

'I know you can. I'm just trying to be nice because I can see I've pissed you off. Again. But it's up to you – I can see my bus coming. Shall I get on it and we both go home feeling shitty or shall we bury the hatchet and have some nearly undrinkable chocolate, whoever buys it?'

Ariel struggled with herself. She knew Pat was right and she definitely didn't want to part ways feeling this bad. But... She tried for a smile and gave her customary shrug. But she was no match for Pat and gave in to her friend's bear hug as they changed direction and headed for the cafeteria.

EIGHTEEN

Saturday

Dear Will,

An epiphany! I keep asking you what you'd think about various situations in my life, which plenty of people would say is utterly pathetic, and they may very well be right.... (Not my life, that's certainly not pathetic, but that I need to know what you think about it.) Then last Monday night I had a dream about not being able to find the notes I needed in my notebook. I knew the answer to the assignment question was there, but I went through the book – which was now my journal – page after page after page and couldn't find what I was looking for. Even though I knew it was there; I could see it in my mind's eye. When I got to the end of the book a FISH slithered out, and what colour do you suppose the fish was? Yep, bright red. Amazing, but even more amazing was that it took me two whole days and another, rather similar dream, to get the point: RED HERRING. I'm still working out quite what the red herrings are and what the real issue is that I'm rather conveniently avoiding.

Ellen wants to know why I'm 'so sad-looking', which is a reasonable question, given how lovely my life really is these days. Yes, I know I'm in a bit of a tizz about Patrick (but it's actually a pretty happy tizz) and yes, I'm uncomfortable about Joy Parker and Eric Pearson, but there's nothing I can do about that. As for Pat, she's actually the gadfly that keeps forcing me to look at things I don't want to look at.

Of course I've thought about Pat, the Parkers, Patrick, even Paul (what a lot of Ps in my life all of a sudden!) and the college courses. But they, of course, are all various red herrings. What is, deep down, troubling me, is my changing feelings about you and our shared life. In fact, YOUR life altogether.

For example: How could you forget your original name? You couldn't – you just didn't want me to know it. I wonder why.

And that thought leads to another realization: there were other things, many other things, that you didn't want me to know about. Including how you pretended not to recognise my need for a Dad because your own needs were very different, and about as far from paternal as it's possible to be. You somehow managed to get me to collude with that, too. You didn't want me to look at it and frankly I haven't wanted to look at it either. Yet today, before I wrote this, I looked back at what I've written recently in my journal and my questions – whilst not exactly screaming out at me – are very definitely there in what I've written to you. Mostly about the difference between our needs. I'm not sure you 'called forth my best' and now I wonder if I called forth yours. I know I tried, but you wanted something quite different, didn't you?

Why, Will? Was your obsession with the Durants so all-consuming that you didn't care who or what you sacrificed to maintain your delusion? Yet you seemed to genuinely care for and about me. What am I not seeing? What 'red herring' will pop up my dreams now?

And actually, it's one's PRESENCE that 'calls forth' the other's best, according to Epictetus. Not necessarily anything one does. That's an interesting thought to get me through a bit of a turmoil-y time tonight.

•

Ariel made a herculean effort to set aside the anguish she'd felt as she'd written in her journal that afternoon, and set off, early, in a determinedly cheerful mood for her babysitting evening at the Parkers. Somehow her conversation with Ellen had made it easier for her to stop thinking about Joy and Eric's behaviour and this, in turn, allowed the return of her enjoyment of the whole Parker family. She hoped she was in time to see the boys before they went to bed.

'Air-rull!' Nigel ran to the door to hug her, older brother Graham not far behind.

'Oh great,' Joy faked annoyance, 'now they'll never go to

bed. You'll have to come up and read them their story.'

'I'd like that. And if you want, I'll tuck them in for sleep so you and Clive can leave whenever you're ready.'

'Thanks, I accept that with pleasure.' Joy kissed her sons, put on her coat and hurried to the door. 'Clive can't come tonight – he's had to work late, so I'm meeting Eric instead. See you later.'

Ariel tried to pretend to herself that she hadn't heard that and gave her all to the stories. Not surprisingly the little boys were reluctant to let her stop, so she made herself calm down and read a final story in what she hoped was a sleep-inducing tone. And sure enough, by the time she'd finished Graham was deeply asleep, mouth slightly open as always, and Nigel's eyelids were drooping heavily. She kissed his soft little cheek and tiptoed from the room.

Downstairs she stood in front of the fire and pondered. Maybe she hadn't heard Joy correctly. Maybe Joy hadn't said Eric, maybe she'd said...what? what could she have possibly said that sounded like 'I'm meeting Eric instead'?

She considered phoning Ellen but was suddenly anxious that somehow her call would be recorded so Joy or Clive could hear it later. She knew, logically, that wasn't possible, but couldn't make herself risk it. Besides, what help could Ellen be anyway? And in any case, her loyalty to Joy Parker would make it difficult for her to talk about it to anyone, even Ellen who seemed to understand her feelings about it all.

She made herself a cup of tea and tried to think about her latest assignment from the Philosophy and Logic class: she was to make up a profound quote that brooks no argument. She didn't even know where to begin. Pat had created hers already: Man is biodegradable. 'Sounds more like a bumper sticker, though,' she'd laughed at herself, 'but that's the best I can do. Or all I'm willing to do, anyway.' Once again, Ariel was filled with admiration for her friend's ability to say or do a thing and not agonise over it for weeks on end afterwards. How had she learned to do that? And could she, Ariel, somehow learn to do it, too?

No Patrick this evening. He'd told her that last week; he was in Manchester on a course. She couldn't decide if his absence made things better or worse. Probably better, she decided; she could hardly discuss with him her distress at his sister's behaviour.

She washed her tea mug and tried to settle with Joy's latest cookery magazine. The list of ingredients was incredibly uninspiring so she began, in her head, composing a letter (that she knew she would never send) to the magazine, taking them to task and offering to supply a much more interesting list for their next issue. She was just beginning to write the list when Clive arrived home.

'Oh, hello Ariel, I didn't expect to find you here. Has Joy gone shopping then?'

'She didn't say. She said you were working late, but she didn't say where she was going.' True. She'd said she was meeting Eric, but she hadn't said where. For all Ariel knew they had both gone shopping.

'Well, that's a conundrum. I can't really take you home unless she's here, but it seems a shame to keep you…'

'Oh I can catch the bus. Don't worry about that.' She screwed up the half-created list of ingredients and threw it into the fire. She got her coat, crossing her fingers that Clive wouldn't protest or ask any other questions – and that she wouldn't have to wait too long for the next bus.

'Let me pay you then – for the whole evening of course. It's not your problem that it was a short night.' Clive gave her the usual amount and held open the door for her to leave. 'Many thanks then. See you next week.'

Ten minutes later she was on the number 80 bus and forty-five minutes after that she was home. Ellen and Howard were out, so she rummaged through the freezer for an almond Magnum and went up to her room.

'Why am I so upset about all this?' she whispered to herself in the mirror. She moved to the window and began watching for cars as she ate the Magnum. 'One going to Hexham…two going to Hexham…one going away from Hexham…three-one to Hexham …'

•

'Who was your best friend before me, Ariel?'

'Will. I thought I'd told you.'

'No, I mean besides Will.' Pat scooped up the whipped cream she'd had added to her hot chocolate and slowly sucked it off the spoon. 'Yum…I could do this every day, except I'd put on half a stone in no time at all. And I'm noh-ravvin-that, as they say. No, I mean proper friend.'

'Nobody. I didn't have any other friends, only Will. I thought I'd told you. We were all in all to one another.'

Pat looked quizzically at her. 'All-in-all?' mockingly. 'Except you weren't. You didn't have sex with him you said. So you weren't all-in-all to him. What about other friends?'

'Honestly, there weren't any. We never saw any other people. Will said I was all he'd ever needed or wanted and actually, that's how I felt about him. I never even thought about having any other friends.'

'Well what about his family? Or even neighbours? You can't have seen nobody.'

'His family was all dead and there weren't any neighbours. And we did see nobody – we liked it that way. We worked together; we had a project that we worked on together, we didn't need any other people. We were writing important things together. And when we weren't working, we did other things, things for fun as well as chores and things, together. You should be able to understand that. After all, it's what you and Glyn are like.'

'Ariel, that's just plain freaky. You do see that, don't you? Glyn's my boyfriend and near enough my own age. He was thirty-something and you were what? Ten? Twelve? Thirteen?

I've lost the thread here, what with your missing birth certificate and the fake birthdays. But even if you were nineteen or twenty – which you certainly were not – that was a huge age difference. And for that matter, if Patrick is a solicitor already, he's not exactly a teenager, is he? You do seem to have a thing for much older men. Freud would have something to say about that, methinks.'

Ariel didn't know how to answer. She felt attacked by Pat. Life with Will had seemed so right at the time – how could she get Pat to see that now? She couldn't even begin to respond to the comment about older men in general and Patrick in particular. She shrugged, and said nothing.

But Pat wouldn't let go. 'Well what about his friends then, friends from before you?' Silence. 'Oh, he didn't have any, did he? Oh Ariel... Was it really just the two of you, day in, day out, all by yourselves, avoiding the world and working on some whacky project? That is SO weird.'

'It wasn't a whacky project. And it didn't feel weird, Pat. Honestly it didn't.'

'Well it accounts for a lot, if you ask me. I've always said you seem as if you've been locked away for ten years – you're SO out of touch with life.'

'You said five years actually,' Ariel defended the only thing she could.

'Five, ten, what's the fucking difference? If you ask me, you've been abused, my small but perfectly formed little friend.'

'Well I didn't fucking ask you!' Ariel was furious. 'And if this is what friends do, then I'm glad we didn't have any other friends. She pushed her chair back roughly, grabbed her book bag and stamped angrily out of the cafeteria.

'You're supposed to say "with friends like you, who needs enemies?"' Pat called after her.

'Why don't you put that in for your profound quote?' Ariel shouted back, not quite oblivious to the eight or ten other students in the cafeteria, all watching the scene with great interest; and making her feel all the more furious.

She strode angrily to the bus stop where she waited, breathing heavily, until her bus came. 'Damn Pat,' she muttered under her breath as she boarded. 'Damn her and her stupid interfering questions. Who does she think she IS to question my relationship with Will who was as close to perfect as a friend as any human being can be. Unlike her.'

•

Not surprisingly, sleep was hard to come by. All her usual techniques – thinking about the important things in her life, for example – were useless. Everything was connected with Pat – or with Will, and therefore, now, back to being connected with Pat. She tried sorting them into categories in her mind: Sudoku, crosswords, birding, all connected with Will; college, the Parkers, even – by extension – Patrick, with Pat. And thinking about Pat always led back to thinking about Will, which led back to the row they'd had today. There was nothing in her life that wasn't contaminated by one or both of them. Not even C S Lewis, because he was connected with grief, which was connected with Will, which led her back to Pat and the row.

Black and white thinking! She heard Mr Woods' voice in her head. 'Okay then, YOU come up with something that isn't connected with either of them,' she challenged him, and turned over from her back to her front. Again.

Well, yes, there was the Ethics class. Pat had no real connection with that. Oh fuck! She pulled herself up and banged her forehead on the headboard. She hadn't gone to class this afternoon – she'd been so consumed with her rage at Pat that she hadn't given it a thought as she'd gone storming to the bus stop. Damn and double-damn. She'd never catch up. Because it was a short course it was incredibly intensive, so missing two whole hours, even if she got the notes from somebody, would leave a huge hole in her learning. It had been a bit of a struggle to keep up anyway; now she'd never get it.

So she wouldn't go tomorrow. Or ever again. Decision made.

But there was no relief in the decision. Only fury, at herself as well as at Pat, who was undoubtedly to blame for all this.

Onto her back again. How about P&L? She wouldn't have to give that up, would she? She could bunk off tomorrow and still catch up; she knew that. Mr Woods himself would probably bring her up to date in ten minutes. And by not going, she wouldn't have to face Pat, and that was an attractive proposition. So she'd go birding tomorrow instead. And do her absolute best to keep thoughts of Will out of it. Unless somehow such thoughts could be soothing.

He'd introduced her to birding, but it had been her passion for the activity, combined with a rare hoopoe landing in their garden, that had brought about their downfall. In an unusual act of rebellion she'd disobeyed him and contacted the BTO, who had sent someone out to verify the sighting. That, and her talking to the postman on a daily basis, had sent Will into a furious panic which had resulted in their leaving the area for weeks until he'd felt safe enough to settle somewhere else. And somehow, during their exile, the relationship had deepened sexually, to the point that she had impulsively kissed him 'properly' before he left to get back their cats so they could leave forever. The kiss, which had been like nothing she had ever experienced before or since (and certainly not with Ivor) had evidently thrilled Will too, making him uncharacteristically careless about turning out of their driveway, and he had been hit by an oncoming SUV and killed instantly. And if none of this had happened she wouldn't be falling out with Pat – who wouldn't even be in her life anyway.

All her fault, not Pat's after all. There was no getting around it. If she hadn't been interested in birding, she would never have noticed the hoopoe. Then she wouldn't have contacted the BTO and Will wouldn't have felt they had to leave the area (she probably would still have chatted to the postman though…she liked talking to him about 'her dad'. Though no, to be fair, she was only at their post-box because she was out birding in the early mornings). And if she hadn't kissed him so sensuously, and agreed with him that they would consummate their love that very night, he wouldn't have been so mindless as he drove out of the driveway. And if she hadn't insisted on taking the cats – who had been in care with their former owner whilst Will and Ariel had travelled around – he wouldn't have been going out of the drive. And none of this would have happened.

She turned over again. 'Got my assignment statement then: "it's all my fault". Nobody could argue with that.'

NINETEEN

Saturday

Life is shit. I'm not sleeping, not eating, not concentrating and I don't want to live. And it's all my fault. I missed Ethics on Tuesday (so haven't been since – and won't now) and I skipped P&L on Wednesday, so I didn't have to deal with Pat. It took all my courage to go on Friday and she wasn't there! How very dare she?!!! I don't know if she was there on Wednesday or not. I want her to have been there. I wanted her to see I wasn't there, and to worry about me and our supposed friendship. I'm not worried about her though. I don't care. I'm too busy trying to catch up with what I missed. And struggling to not care that I've abandoned the Ethics course. I haven't told Mr Woods and I don't suppose I'll tell Paul on Monday, either.

And now it's babysitting night. I'm not sure I can deal with that. Deal with Joy and Eric, is what I mean. I'm not even sure I want Patrick to call round. I'm not exactly good company and certainly have nothing nice to talk about.

Ellen asked me again if I'm all right. Well, no. But I said I was. I'm not in the mood to talk even to her about any of this. She probably wouldn't understand anyway. As for Howard: don't make me laugh! I don't know if he even knows who Will is! (I meant to write Pat, not Will. But it all amounts to the same thing.)

And actually, I feel as if I've fallen out with Will, too. My last 'letter' to him in my journal was pretty confrontational. Obviously I didn't know at the time that I'd be needing his comfort and support tonight. And that's a joke, too. He's dead! (But writing to him when I've been in a better frame of mind has been soothing, I can't deny that.)

Well, anyway, I think I'll go early so I can be with Graham and Nigel. That would be comforting. They (whoever 'they' is) say you should never work with children or animals. 'They' are wrong: you can never trust anything else; children and animals are the only real things and you can always rely on them to be there for you.

•

Ariel's black mood lifted the instant she walked in the Parkers' door and was set-upon by Graham and Nigel. The latter's 'Air-rull!' was so soothing that she made an immediate decision to stay Ariel, to change her name by deed poll when she was able, and to abandon both Jessica and Jecca for ever. 'Well,' she thought, 'at least that's one thing sorted.'

Clive was there and all seemed normal and affectionate as usual between him and Joy. She helped Joy bath the children and then sat with them as Joy read their story. She was touched – and further calmed – by Graham's falling asleep against her and really didn't want him to be detached and slid into his own bed.

She went downstairs with Joy, pleased at how warm she felt towards her, but at the same time thinking she ought not to be. 'Oh well, it's really nothing to do with me,' she thought. And if it wasn't actually happening right in front of her, maybe she could put it out of her mind and enjoy the Parker family as before.

After they'd left, she realised she hadn't brought either her journal or her notebook, so was at a bit of a loose end. She flipped through Joy's cookery magazines but couldn't find anything to hold her attention. She drifted into the bathroom to look at herself in the mirror.

'I seem to spend a lot of time just hanging about, waiting, in this place,' she muttered. 'And just what am I waiting for this time?'

She returned to the lounge with a mug of tea and decided she might as well think about her assignment, even though she didn't have her book with her. She couldn't concentrate though. Pat's 'bumper sticker' offering kept popping into her mind, followed of course by thoughts of Pat and how angry she, Ariel, was with her erstwhile friend. She flipped through a woman's magazine that Joy had left on the sofa and read her horoscope. *All may seem lost but remember, Pisces, you are actually two fishes, each swimming in the opposite direction. The key will be to decide which way to go and which way to ignore. Chances are good with this week's full moon in Neptune that you'll make the right decision.* Hm, mildly encouraging, though as she felt at the moment, she thought the chances she would make the right choice were actually pretty slim. At the moment she wasn't even clear what the two options might be. Should she read the Taurus horoscope as well? No, her birthday was not the tenth of May; it was the fifth of March. Will had arbitrarily changed it to the May date because that's when Ariel Durant's birthday was. But if you believed in horoscopes at all you'd know that the whole point was that the actual day you were born was the important thing. So no, she wouldn't read the offering for Taurus. Mind you, she'd read somewhere that Robert Louis Stevenson had 'gifted' his 13th November birthday to a little girl who had been born on Christmas Day because he'd felt so sorry for her. But that had been an act of kindness; Will had changed her birthday to suit his own needs. The fifth of March had been fine for her; the tenth of May meant nothing.

Reading her horoscope reminded her that her sixteenth birthday was not far away. Ellen had asked her that morning what sort of a celebration she'd like, saying that sixteen was actually a rather significant milestone. At the time she had been in no mood to think of celebrations and to be honest, she wasn't feeling much like it now. And what was so special about being sixteen anyway? (Well, for one thing, she could have married Will. In Scotland. If he hadn't been killed.)

And she could change her name by deed poll without involving Howard. That was good. Wasn't it? At the moment she wasn't sure she wanted to stay connected with Will Dee. But on the other hand, she didn't feel particularly connected with Howard Pike, either. Maybe she should come up with something entirely of her own choosing. Hm, that was something to think about.

She found a pencil and ripped a sheet off Joy's shopping list pad and began writing down possibilities. She decided to assume, for the moment anyway, that she would retain Ariel ('mostly because of you, sweet Nigel'), so now it was a matter of working out what would go nicely with that. She wondered where the Parkers kept their telephone directory; that would be a good place to start looking.

Patrick arrived as she reached the Cs. So far she had decided against anything beginning with A, not really wanting A A for a set of initials. In fact, she probably wouldn't want any vowel. From the Bs she had listed, very tentatively, Barley, Blakemore, Bosworth and Brownleigh. A maximum of four from each letter would be plenty; that would give her over eighty to choose from.

She told him what she was doing, though not why in any great detail. 'What a wonderful idea!' he said. 'Wish I could help, but there's no way I would choose a name for you. I've always thought that the burden of choosing children's names would weigh very heavily. But perhaps less so if I remember that the children could always do what you are considering doing, and change their names if they want to.'

She made them each a tea and told him about her assignment. He was amused at Pat's effort and said he didn't see why it shouldn't pass muster with Mr Woods. Ariel hoped he'd make some suggestions for her but he seemed determined to avoid it. Part of her appreciated that, but only part of her. He expressed his confidence that she would come up with a 'cracker'; she only hoped he was right.

'Less than two months to the first cricket match of the season,' he said, stretching his long legs to the fire. 'Is Joy right when she says you've agreed to do tea-duty at the home fixtures with her?'

Ariel felt cheered immediately. Here, at last, was something that had nothing to do with Pat. 'Yes, she is. I'm really looking forward to it.'

'Me too. I say, Ariel, do you know anything about scoring? I mean keeping score officially? We badly need a second scorer, though of course if you did that, you couldn't cut sandwiches or slice buns with the tea ladies.'

'I've never done it, but I'm sure I could learn to pretty quickly. I'd like to.' Her semi-cheered up mood lifted even more.

'Actually, that might work out perfectly. We need the extra scorer for the away games and you wouldn't be on tea patrol then; their ladies would be doing it. Oh do say yes. I'll give you a complete tour of the scoring book and you could ride with us, Eric and me, to wherever we go.'

Not even the mention of Eric plunged her back to the depths. After all, she'd liked Eric, so sharing a car with him and Patrick would be fine if it happened. Probably easier than riding with Patrick alone really, though why she'd suddenly thought that was beyond her. He was easy to be with.

The evening passed pleasantly, with Patrick still there, drinking cider, when Joy and Clive came home.

'Can you give me a lift, too, Clive?' Patrick asked. 'I came on the bus but would appreciate a more comfortable ride home.' He turned to Ariel. 'My car's having its MOT and it's not going well at the moment.'

Ariel started to get in the back of the car, but Patrick held open the front door for her and insisted he would ride in the back. Clive said they would drop her first as Clive lived further away.

'Is this absolutely where you live?' Patrick said as they pulled up at Howard and Ellen's gate. 'Ah, I sense your astonishment – that's what Daisy Buchanan says to Jay Gatsby when she sees his pile. The Great Gatsby – ever read it?'

She shook her head, but knew that she would order it immediately and finish it by next Saturday.

'I like that line because it's so not how people really speak. I've been dying for an opportunity to use it legitimately.'

Ariel was enchanted; this was the kind of conversation she loved. 'I suppose if you change "absolutely" to "really" – which means the same thing – then it makes better sense.'

'It does indeed. I shall now spend the week finding words to use in off-beat ways and get on everybody's nerves in the office.'

He got out of the car and walked up the path with her, his

hand under her elbow. 'Goodnight, Ariel. Hope to see you next week – I'll bring the scoring book to show you.'

She smiled and went inside where, after closing the door carefully behind her, she let out a soft whoop of happiness. 'What a change since I left here at half past five,' she whispered. 'Life is definitely looking up again.'

Except for Pat. Her spirits plummeted once more.

•

'Thought any more about your birthday, Jessica?' Ellen was drifting aimlessly round the kitchen in her dressing gown, clearly enjoying the fact that it was Sunday and therefore a day off.

'Not the celebratory part. I'm pretty sure I don't want any kind of party; I don't know enough people well enough for that.'

'Your father and I have talked about taking you out for a special meal but I've been thinking how that might not be special for you – we three eat together pretty often anyway. So...I'm wondering if you'd like us to treat you and your friend Pat to an event. A day at a spa, say, or of course a special meal somewhere.'

'Oh dear. It's a lovely idea, Ellen. Thank you for that, but Pat and I don't seem to be friends any more.'

'What?' Ellen sat down heavily at the table. 'What's happened? If you'd like to tell me, that is. I don't want to pry.'

'You're not prying. I probably need to tell somebody real. I mean, writing about it in my journal doesn't seem to be helping.'

'Come on, let's get dressed and go out for lunch ourselves. Then you can tell me what's going on and I'll see if I can help.'

Ariel was ready before Ellen, so spent a few minutes looking through their telephone directory for possible names.

'Who are you looking up?' Ellen reappeared, ready to go.

'I'll tell you that at lunch, too.' Ariel was feverishly working out in her mind what she wanted to tell Ellen and what she very much needed to keep to herself. She needed advice from Ellen on how to get back on friendly terms with Pat and she'd also like to float the idea of the name change, too. She had realised lately that Ellen was not an automatic information conduit to her father, though if the occasion warranted it, she might prove useful as a sort of stalking horse, preparing the ground, as it were, for Ariel to tell him something. She wondered whether this would be devious behaviour, or simply an intelligent way to deal with tricky things. She'd ask Pat. Oh, no, she couldn't. They weren't speaking.

●

They set off with no particular destination in mind, but quickly found an attractive country pub offering Sunday lunch.

'What about Howard?' Ariel had asked, as they drove away from the house.

'He can make himself a sandwich. He's happily watching the football anyway, so he can eat off a tray, and we can have a more substantial meal this evening. He seemed quite content when I told him we were off for a ladies' lunch in the country. That's not really his thing anyway.'

They settled into a table for two near the fire and looked at the menu board. 'You're as near sixteen as makes no difference, so if you want something to drink...' Ellen looked enquiringly at her.

'No thanks. Mrs Parker usually leaves me a bottle of cider and I don't really like it. Patrick – that's her brother – sometimes drops in to chat and he usually drinks it and I have a cup of tea.'

'Have you mentioned Patrick before? I rather think not.'

'Probably not. I haven't really thought there was much to mention until recently and then I'd got so used to not saying anything that I wasn't sure how to start.' Ariel smiled ruefully.

'Not that there's anything much to say about him now, really, and there's certainly nothing wrong with him. I quite like him, actually. And,' she rushed on, 'he's asked me to go to his cricket matches this summer and help with the teas or the scoring. Or both.'

'Well, well. Good for you. And good for Patrick!' Ellen sipped her wine. 'So nothing making you unhappy there then?'

'Oh no. No, it's Pat. We keep falling out over…over…I don't know what over really. She asks questions about my time with, you know, that man.'

'Will. You can say his name. I know who you mean.'

'Yes, Will. She doesn't seem to understand what we were doing, but she keeps asking and asking and I don't know what to say anymore. And now we've had what she'd call a flaming row and we aren't speaking. In fact, she wasn't in class on Friday so I can't tell if she's wanting to make up or not.'

'Are you? Wanting to make up?'

'Of course I am! I miss her horribly.'

'So ring her – or go round, and tell her you want to be friends again. Or are you waiting for her to make the first move?'

Ariel thought for a moment. 'No, I don't think I am, but I am scared she'll reject my olive branch and I don't think I could face that.'

'Ah yes, that's a hard place to be. I do understand because I've had the same fears when your father and I have words. So what I usually do is say something like "I'm willing to make up if you are" and see what he says to that.'

'Does that work?' Ariel was fascinated by this insight into the parents' world. She had never imagined them 'having words'.

'Always.' Ellen smiled. 'Well, so far anyway.'

'Okay, maybe I'll try that. But what if she says she isn't

willing? Or just plain blanks me? What do I do then?'

'What I decided to do, only I haven't had to – yet, anyway – is say something really grown up like "well you know where I am when you change your mind".'

'That certainly puts the ball back in their court – but what if they don't ever change their mind?'

'Then this is not a friend for you, Jessie. This is an angry baby in grown-up clothes and you deserve better in a friend.'

'Crikey, you're wise, Ellen.'

'Not always, but thank you. Ah, here's our lunch.'

They ate in companionable silence for a while. Then, 'So that's Pat then; do you want to tell me any more about Patrick…or the Parkers? You've sort of hinted that something was troubling you there.'

'I really love the Parkers, but I'm a bit rattled by how Joy acts with a friend of theirs. I don't want to say much because she asked me not to, but the fact that she asked me not to say anything makes me think it's not all right, the way she is with Eric – he's a friend of Patrick's as well.'

'Hm. Well I won't push – I'm sure you know you can tell me anything you want me to know, and I hope you know you can trust me not to break your confidence. However, as she has asked you not to tell, you probably don't want to break hers. That's hard, Jess. But I can't ask you to do something you don't feel right about.'

'I did sort of talk to Pat about it – I didn't exactly tell her, she seemed to guess from my face when she was asking questions. Or at least she said she did and in any case she knew about Joy and this man. Apparently a lot of people know about them, probably even her husband, Pat thinks.'

Ellen pushed her plate to the side. 'It all sounds quite messy. But on the other hand, if he – Mr Parker – knows and apparently isn't doing or saying anything about it, then who are we to interfere?'

'That's more or less what Pat said. I've sort of accepted that, but it still doesn't sit very well with me. So mostly I try to ignore it and I've promised myself I won't be around them if I don't like how they are with each other. Though – I've just realised – he plays cricket too and Joy Parker has also asked me to help her with the teas, so I'll see them together there.'

'There'll be plenty of other people there too. Including her brother.'

'And her husband. I think Clive plays for the same team.'

'Well I definitely wouldn't worry about it then. In fact, I wouldn't worry any way. I learned a long time ago that managing my own life is a full-time job; there's no room to get all moralistic about others' lives.'

'I'm sure you're right. Thanks, Ellen. That's really helpful. I feel a bit better about both things now.'

'That's good. Anything else I can help resolve for you? Three for the price of two, today.' Ellen laughed.

'Well, actually, yes. There is something else I want to mention.' Ariel took a deep breath.

'Fire away.'

'Well. You know how while I was with Will I was Ariel Dee?'

'Yes?'

'And after he…he was killed, everybody made me go back to Jessie Pike – or Jessica Pike?'

Ellen nodded.

'Well, I've been thinking about whether I want to be Jessica Pike or whether I'd like to do a deed poll thing when I turn sixteen and officially become Ariel Dee.' She drew a deep breath and looked at Ellen, trying to gauge her reaction.

'Do I gather that when you're sixteen you won't need your parents' permission?'

'That's what it says online. But the thing is, I don't know now if I want to do that. I do like Ariel, I think I might like to keep that. It's the Dee versus Pike bit I'm struggling with now.'

If Ellen was shocked she didn't show it. Possibly, Ariel thought in the logical part of her brain, because her names weren't involved. Somehow she didn't think Howard would be that calm about it.

Ellen looked thoughtful. 'This is such a personal thing that I honestly don't feel it would be right for me to advise you in either direction. But what I do feel, quite passionately, actually, is that in the end you have to do what you want to do. One's name is absolutely integral to who we feel we are. I didn't much want to become a Pike when I married your father, I didn't want to be "the second Mrs Pike" for starters, but – and probably because he was easy either way – I decided in the end that Pike was better than what I already had: Kreft. I really hated that. Mostly because my middle name is Elizabeth and I got sick and tired of being called EEK. EEP seems quite harmless by comparison. What's your middle name?'

'I haven't got one. Oh, I see, maybe I could have both Jessica and Ariel. I hadn't thought of that. Then I could be whichever one I wanted in any situation. That would resolve the first name part anyway. Oh thanks Ellen, I think you've just done it again!'

Ellen smiled happily and finished her wine. Ariel realised again how much her stepmother had wanted to be helpful and how, for so long, Ariel had kept her at arm's length. She'd been so busy wanting and looking for a father that having a good-enough mother had never entered her thought process.

'Final piece of advice for today then: remember I said a few weeks ago that once you've done something it can be hard to undo it? Well, this is similar: don't rush into the name change because you can always do it, right up to the end of your life, in fact. Don't dash to get it done the second you turn sixteen – unless you're one hundred per cent sure, because you just might change your mind again. And I know, you can simply do another deed poll, but why waste the money? Not to mention having to re-educate everybody again and again,' she smiled.

'I know you're right. And I know I've been having second thoughts about it or obviously I would have just gone ahead. And that's why I've been looking in the phone book for possible second names so I don't have Pike or Dee.'

Ellen nodded solemnly. 'Yes, that's very telling. You started feeling you had to be Dee, not so much because you didn't want to be Pike. And now you're not sure. Okay, then please, I implore you, don't do anything in a tearing hurry. Let it sit for a while until you wake up one day just absolutely knowing what you want to do. And that's what will happen, I'm sure of that.'

'You're very wise Ellen. And I'm learning from you all the time. Thank you – and thank you for my lunch, too. If you're nearly ready....I think I might ring Pat this afternoon and start that ball rolling. Even though she's probably out with Glyn, but I could leave her a message and I don't want to wait any longer.'

'Good girl! I'm very proud to be your stepmother.' Ellen linked her arm through Ariel's and they walked to the car, each relishing, Ariel felt, an awareness of a new deepening of their relationship, and both obviously feeling very happy about it.

TWENTY

Saturday

Dear Will,

Better week! What a brick Ellen has turned out to be – I had no idea. Well, I never gave her a chance really. But she doesn't seem to hold it against me.

And Pat and I are back together, that feels so HUGE. I absolutely HATED (and that's not a word I really use much, if at all; I try hard not to do hate) not being friends with her. I followed Ellen's advice and asked her – left a message on her phone as she was, predictably, out with Glyn when I rang – saying exactly what Ellen had suggested. Ten minutes later (a difficult ten minutes, I have to say) she rang back saying 'OF COURSE I WANT TO BE FRIENDS, YOU NINNY! Can't talk now, see you on Tuesday – come on the earlier bus.'

So I did and she was waiting at the bus stop. I've never had such a bear hug in my entire life! Oh I do love her and feel so relieved that we aren't not-speaking any more. I thought we ought to unpick how we'd fallen out but she wasn't having any of it. 'NO. We draw a line under it and move on. It's over and in the past. End of.' Perhaps not ideal for our future relationship, but who knows? Evidently that's how she and Glyn manage their disagreements and it certainly works for them. She did say she'd try not to probe any more about my life with you Will him, and I said I'd try not to be so touchy about it. I think you'd be proud of me, Will.

And we both got an A for our brooks-no-argument statements. And yes, she did use her 'bumper sticker' one. Mr Woods drew a smiley face beside the A on her paper and wrote 'thanks for the chuckle'. My final effort, after much agonising and crossing out and ripping up, was: 'It is not possible to come up with a saying that cannot be disagreed with at some level'. Mr Woods wrote on my paper 'I didn't expect you to bottle it,

Ariel, but of course, you're dead right – or I'd be out of a job. A (Reluctantly).' In class he read out a few others' offerings that he'd awarded an A, but not mine and not Pat's. When she asked him why not (I would never had dared) he said he didn't want to encourage her – or me! I'm not sure what to make of that and will, if I get the chance, ask Patrick what he makes of it.

Yes. Feeling better all round today. Looking forward to babysitting and going early again so I can put the boys to bed. Sometimes I think I ought to be paying the Parkers rather than the other way around.

Pat thought Jessica Ariel Whatever, 'though not "Whatever", or your initials would be JAW!' would be better than dropping either name entirely. She has a point – Jessica Ariel Pike would be JAP, which isn't much better. Jessica Ariel Dee would be JAD which is probably harmless. Oh, maybe the other way then: Ariel Jessica Whatever – you can't really make a word that way. Something else I can discuss with Patrick if he comes round tonight.

Pat says he's obviously not 'taken' or he wouldn't be spending his Saturday evenings babysitting with me. Good point. I hope. At least I think I do.

Pat likes Ellen's idea of her and me going for a spa day and suggested Hopton Manor because, she says, a posh lunch is thrown in. It may be more than Ellen and Howard were thinking of spending, but I will mention it. I love the idea of a special day out with Pat.

Not sure why I've crossed out the Will bits when I'm obviously writing this entry for him. Oh dear, will I ever understand myself?

•

'Have you dropped the Ethics course, Jessica? Paul squinted over his glasses at her.

'I suppose I have. I missed one and felt I'd never catch up, so

I haven't been for ages now.'

'I see. But you can't just not show up, you know. You'll need to officially withdraw so your college record doesn't have a black mark against you. I'm keeping my eye on your university career, you know.'

'Oh, no, I didn't know that – that I'd have to do something official. I hope it's not too late. How did you know I haven't been going, anyway?'

'Simply that you haven't mentioned it lately. I'm not psychic, or anything modern and magic like that, you know.' He smiled. 'How did you miss one? Were you ill?'

'No, believe it or not I was so consumed with something else that I simply forgot to go and then felt I'd never catch up. It's terribly intense, I've got sheets and sheets of notes from each session, you know.' Ariel knew she could never even begin to explain to Paul what had happened.

'That's college – and later – university life, I'm afraid. I'm fairly easy-going and soft on you, and you love Jack Woods' class, but it won't always be that way. If you are serious about a university place you'll have to buckle down and do things you don't always feel like doing.'

She felt chastened. And ashamed of herself. She'd never not enjoyed learning before. Anything Will had wanted to teach her had been very welcome to her. And Paul had never been anything other than fully approving and encouraging of everything she did. She had no idea she had crossed a boundary and was actually in trouble – or could be. 'I'm so sorry,' she said humbly.

'It's a salutary lesson – and a cheap one. But be sure you learn from it.'

'I will. I will, I promise.' She meant it. But it rankled all day.

•

'Before we start enjoying this, I need to get something off my chest, Pat.' They were at the Hopton Manor Spa the day after Ariel's sixteenth birthday.

'Am I going to like it? If not, don't tell me. This is my day out too, remember.'

'It's not even about you – you narcissist! No, it's about dropping the Ethics course,' and she told Pat, as word for word as she could remember, of her conversation with Paul, though not why she had missed the class in the first place. She would do that another time, she promised herself. If the opportunity arose.

'He'll get over it. And I think what you need to learn from it is that you mustn't take things to heart so much. You can be sure he's forgotten about it – and you've done the necessary now with no harm done. Lighten up, Ariel. And get your kit off so we can get into the sauna and sweat ourselves silly.'

Ariel did as she was urged, feeling relieved at Pat's casualness. Sitting in the heated cabin she pondered the similarities in Pat and Ellen, both of whom gave such good advice and were so helpful to her with the problems of living, but yet were so very different in their attitude. At least, on the surface they seemed to be; in fact they were often saying the same things but in different ways. What could she learn from that, she wondered. She decided not to ask Pat, realising that her friend was not in any mood for profound or philosophical conversation today. As she had often said, she didn't really do 'deep thinking'; the P&L course absorbed all her energies on that score.

Somewhat to her surprise, Ariel was able to relax and enjoy a pampering day and being with Pat. After the sauna they each had full-body massages; Pat with 'stones' and Ariel with 'heated bamboo' so they could compare the experience. After a light and healthy lunch ('you'd think they'd at least give us a nourishing gin and tonic,' Pat grumbled) they separated for their next experience. Ariel had chosen a mudpack facial while Pat had an Indian head massage. They ended their day with a manicure and a pedicure – and lots of giggling, as they sat side by side in reclining chairs. An end-of-day swim had been suggested, but neither felt she had enough energy, so they sat in the warmth of the conservatory, sipping lemongrass tea and waiting until Ellen collected them at six o'clock.

'I'll bet we smell delicious,' Pat sniffed her inner arm. 'Glyn's going to enjoy this.'

'I got samples of the perfumes,' Ariel said, 'loads of it, so you can have some and I can give some to Ellen, too.' She felt completely content and there was still her evening at the Parkers with – probably – Patrick, to come.

'If I ask you a question will you promise not to snap my head off?'

Ariel took her time responding. 'Depends what the question is. And to be fair, I don't snap your head off automatically, even when you ask about touchy subjects.'

'True. All right, let me phrase it another way: if I ask you something not about Will, can you stay calm?'

Ariel nodded and waited, somewhat anxiously despite what she'd said to Pat.

'It's not loaded. I just want to ask how you're feeling about Jecca these days. I notice I'm not often – if ever – calling you that and I also notice you haven't said anything, so I'm just wondering...and you'll please notice that I'm trying to be ultra-sensitive.'

'Good question, really. I had sort of noticed – about you being sensitive – thank you – and about Jecca, but that hasn't had an impact on me either way. I suppose that means I'm not that attached to it as a name.

'Want me to drop it?'

'Yes, I think so. If I stay as Jessica, Ariel Jessica something, I will always have the option of Jecca, as well as Jess, Jessie, and probably more.'

'Like Sicca?' Pat laughed. 'Oh, sorry, don't be offended.'

'I'm NOT. Don't act as if I'm uber-touchy all the time.'

'Okay. Here's a test then: how old is your Patrick? And I'm only asking out of nosiness, not to hound you about "older men" or anything like that. I've told you Glyn is three years older than me, and that suits me fine. He's done with school and college, such as it was – he dropped out – and has Life Experience. That's quite a turn-on for me. And I like being taken care of.'

'I think he's 23 but I'm not entirely sure. I'm trying to find a way to find out but I'm nervous about asking Joy Parker; she was pretty quick to see why I asked her what her maiden name was and, like you, teased me about that.'

'Of course she did!' Pat laughed. 'Why go round the houses anyway? Why not just ask Patrick?'

Ariel had no answer for that.

'If he's 23 then that makes him seven years older than you,' Pat mused. 'That's supposed to be lucky in some cultures. The ideal apparently is for the woman to be half the man's age plus seven, so if you'd met him when you were 21 and he was 28 then bingo! My brain can't work out how old he should be now, for you to be spot on. Maths and I don't get along. Two plus two can make anything they bloody-well like as far as I'm concerned. Just so long as they're having a jolly old time together.'

Ariel struggled. 'I need pencil and paper I think. But let's see, if he's 23 now, half that is eleven and a half, plus seven is eighteen and a half. No, doesn't work out right. Oh well. Here's Ellen, anyway.'

TWENTY-ONE

Sunday

Lovely, lovely day yesterday at the spa with Pat (whose birthday present to me has been 'delayed', she says. Whatever that means.) There was one demi-semi-touchy moment but I think we got past it. I mustn't be so sensitive. But perhaps she shouldn't be so insensitive? I don't know, I have no other experience of friends, so I can't tell if she's a bit much or if I am. I think we're trying very hard to meet in the middle though.

I don't know if she asked me about Patrick's age to get me thinking. Probably not, she's more straightforward than that. Though we do have this sort of pact to not go onto sensitive ground... Oh, I don't want to go into that now. I'm feeling too content.

Patrick commented on how 'well' I looked, so I told him about the day at the spa and that it was for my birthday. He said I ought to have told him so he could have brought something special for us to share. So I astonished myself and asked him when his birthday is: the twenty-fourth of August. That's a long time to wait. We may not be... be what? What ARE we? In any case, whatever it is, we may not be it by then. Oh, that's not a happy thought! Anyway, he'll be 23, so he's only six and a half years older than me. Not that it makes any difference, but at least I know. (And it's not Pat's 'lucky' seven.)

He brought up the cricket again and showed me how to keep score in an official scoring book. I think I can do that. I'd have to watch everything very carefully and concentrate ALL the time, but that's why they have two scorers, I suppose. One from each side. Patrick said the lady who does it for his team doesn't want to do the away matches this year, which is why they need someone else of course.

Even having dropped the Ethics course (officially!), I'm very pleased with my life and outlook for the coming months. Summer stretches out most appealingly. Except that the P&L course will end in another month. I shall miss that very much. So I need to decide if I want to tackle the Ethics course again and/or something else. But not today. I'm too mellow to stir up my mind today. After I've written in here I'll finish my P&L assignment (on Absolutes – not terribly riveting) and then go birding. There won't be much new yet, but it will be a nice finish to my birthday weekend. And happy memories of going birding with Will on one of my birthdays – he bought me my own binoculars.

All the better to see you with, my dear….

Why on earth did I say that?

•

'My turn to ask you a question, Pat.'

'Ask away – and let me show you how to answer when your friend asks an undoubtedly harmless question.' Pat grinned at her.

'Do you have other friends – I mean apart from me and Glyn?'

'Of course I do. You can't survive sixth form – or life – without friends. Though as you've probably deduced, I don't do things with them very much these days because of Glyn; and having to do the occasional bit of homework of course. Though one of the advantages of being in the sixth form is that you get what they are pleased to call "study periods". And as I'm not actually studying for anything, I do most of my homework then, including assignments for P&L.'

'What aren't you studying for?' Pat's life was an almost complete mystery to Ariel; she lived in a world that Ariel had absolutely no experience of.

'Oh, A-levels, the sort of exams you need high marks on to get into university. But I'm not going to university so I'm not bothering with the exams either. I shall leave graciously at the end of the summer term – unless they heave me out ungraciously before then. Waste of space and all that.'

'Why are you taking this course, then? From everything you've said, it doesn't seem your kind of thing at all – though I have to say you are doing brilliantly at it.'

'That's why. To show somebody – well everybody, actually – that I'm not a brunette version of the dumb blonde. That's all.'

'Who said that?' Ariel was surprised on two counts: that anyone could think that of Pat, and that Pat would be affected by it.

'One of the sixth form teachers. She's a slimy little toad, actually, and eats wasps for breakfast. I'm getting enormous pleasure out of passing on my marks and reports from the decidedly UN-slimy Mr Woods. But before you ask, no; I'm not signing up for anything else. Job done, as far as I'm concerned. I'll see this lot through and then, much to Glyn's relief, go back to being the bubble-head that I not-so secretly enjoy being, knowing – as I do – that there's a hell of a lot more to me than meets the eye.'

'Pat, you are one of a kind. "Sui generis", if you want the Latin for that.' Ariel smiled in admiration of her friend's honesty. 'And I treasure knowing you.'

'Ta. And now shut up. And from now on, can we just ask each other questions like normal human beings without first asking permission to ask a question?'

'Agreed,' Ariel smiled, 'with relief.'

•

'Would you feel we are taking shameful – or should that be shameless? – advantage of you, Ariel, if we asked you to come early every week? We'd pay you for the extra time of course, but the boys love you so much they are very reluctant to go to bed until they've seen you. So Clive said why don't we take advantage of that and go out earlier? What do you think? Don't be afraid to say no.'

'I don't want to say no! I would be delighted to put them to bed. They are so lovely and loving. I've been thinking actually that I ought to pay you for the privilege.' Ariel felt a surge of happiness and was quite genuine in her response.

'You're a love. You must come to tea then, and take over from there. Sometimes Clive and I will go early, without having tea here, if that's all right with you?'

'Of course it is. Just say what time you want me here and what you need me to do. Are they asleep now?'

'They are, but it wasn't easy – which is what led to Clive and me having this conversation about asking you to come early. I've never had a sitter I could trust with my children awake. So either you are a wonder or I'm getting older and jaded.'

'Both,' Clive chimed in, 'and you're being more realistic.' He began tidying the children's toys as he waited for Joy to get her coat. 'Cricket starts next Sunday, Ariel. I can hardly wait. Highlight of my week, that is and I'll be vice-captain this year. Joy says you're coming to help with teas and things at home matches; that'll be nice for the boys.'

Ariel wondered if he knew she would also be coming to the away matches to help with the scoring. Should she mention it? Or should she let Patrick or Joy take care of that? She was becoming increasingly aware of how seemingly ordinary things took on such a great significance for her because what the Team called her social skills were so underdeveloped. Another legacy from Will, she thought wryly and, not for the first time, felt a flash of envy for Pat's apparent ease with such matters. She told herself she was learning from Pat and would no doubt learn more, but that didn't prevent a sense of irritation with herself. 'Nobody else makes such a big meal of little things like this,' she scolded herself silently.

'I'll pick up the Lego,' she said, aware of Clive's struggle to get under the table for some small pieces. 'I don't mind.'

'You're very kind. I told that social worker what a good soul you are, when she was here last week.'

Ariel was shocked. 'What social worker?' Crikey, were they checking up on her babysitting job now? The shock gave way to fury. 'Did they come asking questions about me? How dare they?'

'I'm sure it's routine,' Joy had reappeared. 'They just want to make sure you aren't coming to any harm, so I think we reassured them we aren't going to corrupt you – and you aren't going to corrupt our boys, either!' She looked at Ariel's face. 'Oy! Just joking!'

As soon as they'd left Ariel phoned home, totally overlooking her previous anxiety about any phone calls being accidentally recorded. Howard answered.

'Did YOU tell the Team about my babysitting? The social workers have been round here checking on me. How DARE they? You shouldn't have told them. They have no right to poke into my life all the time.' She could hardly get the words out.

'Jessica, Jessie-hen, calm down.' She could hear Howard struggling to stay matter-of-fact. 'You know it's part of the deal that we have to let them know what you're doing as long as you're on their Register. And they have to check up to make sure you aren't getting yourself into situations that would be harmful to you. I'm sure they found it all hunky-dory with the Parkers. We'd have heard pretty sharpish if they hadn't. They just have to tick the boxes until you are eighteen. And we have to cooperate with them.'

'Well I wish you'd told ME you'd told them. I don't want them poking into my friendship with the Parkers and Patrick.' As soon as she'd said it she could have bitten off her tongue.

'WHO THE HELL IS PATRICK?' Howard's deliberate calmness abandoned him abruptly.

'Ask Ellen, she knows about him,' sulkily. 'He's Mrs Parker's brother that's all. He comes round sometimes when I'm babysitting but he's not going to abduct me, if that's what you're afraid of. I wish he would though.' She banged down the phone and burst into tears. Damn, damn, damn, it was ruined now. She might have known she wouldn't be allowed to have anything decent for herself: somehow the blasted social workers would interfere and spoil it. She hoped the Parkers hadn't told them about the London trip – or about her going to cricket matches with Patrick. That would be the absolute END!

She paced around the room, not caring how she looked or that she hadn't, as promised, picked up the children's toys. She hoped Patrick wouldn't come tonight. She was in no fit state to talk to him. Damn, damn, a thousand times damn!

She let the doorbell ring a second time before she answered, but it wasn't Patrick, it was Howard and Ellen.

'We were worried about you,' Howard began, 'so we thought we'd come round and see if we could all talk a bit.'

'I don't want to talk to you. You shouldn't have betrayed me to the Team,' and she burst into tears again.

Ellen put both arms around her and held her tightly as she sobbed into her stepmother's shoulder. Howard stood watching, frowning and shuffling his feet in obvious discomfort.

'Wait outside Howard, in the car. Let me talk to her by myself for a few moments.' Ellen untangled one arm and pushed Howard through the door, still holding Ariel in her other arm. 'Come on. Make me a cup of tea and then let's see if we can put this into perspective.' Ellen drew Ariel towards the kitchen where she sat at the table while Ariel filled the kettle. 'I know you're upset and I know we should have mentioned it to you. I'm sorry. We will in future, I promise. We honestly didn't think it was any big deal and were trying to keep life as normal as possible for you. I can see we made a mistake though and I promise – again – I'll tell you whenever there is any contact with the Team.'

Ariel poured the boiling water onto the tea bags and sat down at the table. 'I'm sorry, Ellen. I know you think I'm over-reacting, but it's horrible to be treated like a criminal and to find out that Authority is checking up on me behind my back. I'm trying to have a normal life, too. You wouldn't like it.' She poured milk into her mug and passed the bottle to Ellen.

'No, I wouldn't. And I don't like it for you, but that's how it is. They want to know everything you do and everywhere you go and I suppose a lot of the time they check up on people and places to make sure you aren't coming to any harm. But it won't last for ever. So for now we have to cooperate and be open so they cause the minimum amount of fuss.'

Ariel was silent for several moments, then, 'Did they know about the London thing?'

'Yes. We cleared that with them before you went. And they obviously weren't too concerned because it's only recently that they came to see the Parkers. I'm guessing that was simply pro forma, so they could tick that box.'

Ariel took a deep breath. 'The only trouble there is that it wasn't Mr and Mrs Parker I went with. It was Mrs Parker, Patrick and their friend Eric.'

'Oops.' Ellen pulled a face. 'Your father and I didn't know that either, did we?'

Ariel shook her head slowly, her lips pressed together in a stubborn line.

'I'll make a deal with you, love. If you'll be open and honest with me, I'll do what I can to keep things running smoothly with the Team. But if I don't know what's happening, I can't protect your privacy. And before you ask, no, I won't always feel I have to involve your father. Sometimes what he doesn't know won't hurt him, but you have to trust me. And I have to trust you.' She reached over and took Ariel's hand. 'I'm on your side, you know.'

'I know that. I think I know that, anyway. Okay, I'll do my best though I'm going to hate it. Not because of you, but because it just sucks, as Pat would say.'

'It does. And I would say it too! It very definitely sucks. But let's see what we can do. Deal?'

'Okay. Deal. Oh crikey, is that Patrick coming in with Howard? Oh god I'm not ready for this.' She shot into the bathroom, leaving Ellen to introduce herself to Patrick and hoping they would sort it out for themselves.

●

Waking on Sunday morning Ariel was surprised to find she had slept really well. 'All that emotion!' she decided. 'It's exhausted me.' She lay on her back and thought about the events of the evening. She had to hand it to Ellen–and Howard, too, for that matter – they had been super cool and easy with Patrick, who had been perfectly comfortable with them. Ariel had stayed in the bathroom for as long as she'd dared, dreading the moment when she had to face the three of them together, but she need not have worried. Ellen had been diplomacy personified and even Howard had surprised her with his conversational ease and apparent comfort with the situation.

They had left shortly after Ariel put in her appearance, explaining they had 'just been in the area and thought they'd drop in to see if Jessica needed anything'. That led to some confusion, and Ariel was glad she had told Patrick before about her two names. Under the circumstances, the confusion was minimal, with even Howard referring to her as 'Jessie – Ariel, you know,' more than once. Somehow they managed not to reveal to Patrick what had really prompted the visit – and Ariel's obvious distress – and to his credit he hadn't said anything about her appearance when they left.

But she wanted to tell him, she decided, as she luxuriated in the warm bed, smelling toast and bacon wafting up from the kitchen. She decided she would take a new, more honest, approach to all of her life and she would start with Patrick. Next Saturday, if he came to the Parkers. Ah, no, she'd have to start with Ellen this morning, because next Sunday was the first cricket match and she, Ariel, was going with Joy Parker to help with the teas and the boys. Good, that would show Ellen that she meant what she'd said. She also wanted to thank them both for making the unexpected meeting with Patrick as easy as they had. It can't have been easy for them, she realised, and vowed again to do her bit to make things run as smoothly as possible given the Team's mandatory involvement.

TWENTY-TWO

Saturday

To quote Pat, "life's a flipping roller coaster, so enjoy the ride". Well it is at the moment. I don't know if it's always like that. But somehow something good keeps coming out of all these disasters, and the base note (as they apparently say in the perfume business) still rumbles on as GOOD.

To get the not-goods out of the way first:

--Last week for P&L next week and I don't know what I'm going to do next (aside from missing it horribly). Ah – must bring that up with Paul on Monday and with Mr Woods on Tuesday. Be proactive, Ariel.

--The Team's infuriating involvement in my life. Well, the good thing that's come out of that is the obvious support from not only Ellen but also, somewhat unexpectedly, from Howard. And the pact Ellen and I have to keep things on track in the least painful way. That's going to make things less annoying.

And that's actually all! It's not so much when I write it out. And on the good side is Pat - our friendship keeps getting better, deeper; Ellen (and possibly even Howard) ditto; Patrick ditto? (Possibly, not sure yet); cricket tomorrow; tea and bedtime for the boys tonight; birthday present still to come from Pat (yes? maybe not, must be realistic); SOMETHING this summer to challenge my brain (talk to Paul on Monday).

And perhaps best of all: I don't really think about Will (or the Durants) much any more. Do I feel guilty about not working on the Durants' stuff? I'm not sure I do. And THAT feels very strange, as if I feel guilty about not feeling guilty. I must look back to see what and when I last 'wrote' to Will. I have a feeling I wasn't in the best place in my feelings with him, but at the moment I honestly can't remember. And nor do I want to, today.

Time to make some shortbread to take in as a thank you for Mr Woods on Tuesday, and then off to the Parkers. Yep, life is GOOD.

•

'I enjoyed meeting your parents, Ariel,' Patrick had arrived shortly after she'd got the boys settled in bed and off to sleep. 'It was lovely to see how much Ellen cares for you. And your father, too. You are obviously well-loved.'

'They liked you too.' Had they said that? Ariel couldn't remember it, but it seemed to be the right thing to say. (A tick in the social skills box?) Looking for a slightly safer topic, she asked about arrangements for tomorrow's cricket match.

'Joy's the official tea-lady, she'll talk to you about it. But for the record, the first over is bowled at two o'clock on the dot – and that's a laugh! People still faffing about with the sight screen or having a final fag before taking the field. We'll be lucky if it's bowled by half-past.' Patrick's glorious smile warmed her all over.

'What time is tea then?' Ariel was conscious of her enormous need to Get Things Right, but at the same time desperate not to be seen as what Pat would call—on a polite day—a fusspot.

'Depends. Usually it's after the first side is all out, but sometimes that can happen so quickly you ladies won't even have sliced the cucumbers yet. It's normally somewhere about four o'clock, and we usually wrap it up and head for the pub by about half past six. Will you be joining us there too?'

'Oh, I don't know… It's a bit more complicated for me actually.' Now was the moment, the time to tell Patrick about the restrictions on her life and pray he wouldn't be put off. She took a deep breath and launched in. 'You see, I'm on something called the At Risk Register – not that I've done anything, but… so places I go and people I'm with have to be sort of approved by a social worker. Until I'm eighteen. That's actually why Ellen and Howard were here last week. I was upset because the social worker had been to see Joy and Clive, and I don't think they'll be okay about my being in a pub though I think they're all right

125

about the cricket match. Ellen has talked to them about that and I don't want you to think there's something the matter with me and that I'm a liability....'

'Whoa!' He held up his hand, interrupting her in mid-stream. 'It's all right, Ariel. I know what the At Risk Register is, and Joy has told me a little about you as well, and it's all right. Really.' He smiled and shook his head. 'Of course I don't know the whole story, but you know what? I work for a law firm and things like this are practically everyday occurrences for us. I'm not shocked and I certainly don't think there's anything the matter with you. If anything, I should think it's a right pain in the you-know-what to be monitored like this when you want to be out doing things and having secrets and so on. But you're right, the pub with the cricket lads is probably going to be off-limits as far as the Gestapo social workers are concerned. Which might cramp our style for away games, but we'll work something out. Do you want me to talk to your parents?'

'Oh no!' she was horrified. 'I'll talk to Ellen. She's promised to be the go-between so the Team gets their needs met and I get mine met as far as possible. But thank you, I didn't mean to be so abrupt.'

'You weren't. Let's talk about something else now and then one day, if you want, you can tell me how this all came about. Remember what I said though: you won't shock me. I promise.' Again the smile, and Ariel thought there was probably nothing that smile wouldn't help.

•

'This is our friend Ariel,' Joy ushered her into the kitchen area of the pavilion. 'She's going to help with the teas – or the boys, whichever is the greater need at any given moment.'

The three women working round the table looked up and smiled at her. 'Janet Foster,' said the large middle-aged lady, who was, Ariel could tell instantly, in charge. 'And this is Alice Beck, and that's Maisie... I don't know your last name, Maze – she's Bill Martin's girlfriend.'

'Hello,' Ariel smiled back at them all. 'What shall I do to help?'

'Peel the eggs. That's always the first task, so we can get the egg salad made up. Alice brings them, already hard-boiled, so here, you take them over to the sink and get cracking. Literally.' She laughed a deep throaty chuckle that rumbled down into her lungs and threatened to turn into a cough.

'Looks like you've been snaffled for tea-making duty, Ariel,' Joy began unpacking a box of what looked like cupcakes and Battenbergs. 'So I'll watch the boys until after tea.'

Glad to have something to do, Ariel began peeling the three dozen or so eggs, listening to the women talk as she did. Years of experience at working out what was going on from the available information meant that she pretty quickly worked out that Alice was more or less happily married to Johnnie Beck, and Janet was Derek Foster's mother. Derek was captain, and his father, Janet's husband, was chairman of the Cricket Club and played when they were a man short. She'd have to remember to list him in the scorebook as A N Other if that happened.

The Parkers had driven her there: 'it's on our way really, so we can always pick you up at the end of your road.' Clive had disappeared into the Home dressing room where, she assumed, Patrick and Eric would also be. It wasn't possible to see much of the field from the kitchen but Derek's father, Arthur, popped in regularly to update the ladies on the score.

'He used to be the umpire but he can't stand that long any more,' Maisie explained. 'I think he really misses it, too, so he's sort of taken over the scoreboard as well as keeping us in the picture. Bless him.'

The tea break itself vanished in a blur. Over two dozen hungry men all wanting their mugs filled and refilled and emptying plates as fast as the ladies could fill them meant Ariel hardly had time to notice how striking Patrick looked in his whites. He'd been out third ball, apparently, whilst Eric, his opening partner, had scored an admirable 28 and was needling the slightly rueful Patrick. She did notice – and wished she hadn't – that Joy had ruffled Eric's already tousled hair as she'd refilled his tea mug. Ariel also saw how Joy went to some trouble to work only that end of the table, whilst the other women went wherever there was a need.

When the men's tea was over the ladies ate theirs and then began slowly tidying the table. 'I'll help with the clearing up, Ariel, if you'll take the boys for a walk round the field,' Joy plunged her gloved hands into the washing up bowl and Ariel gathered up the two boys for their walk. With one attached to each hand, she felt a glow of pleasure as she walked down the pavilion steps, past Janet Foster who was coming back up after her post-tea cigarette.

'Now her man's in the field she's okay to help in the kitchen, I suppose.'

'Sorry?' Ariel knew from the older woman's tone that she didn't approve of Joy for some reason, but didn't know how to respond. She also suspected that Janet was not referring to Clive, but to Eric.

This was confirmed when Janet added, 'Clive'll be glad to have you here to keep an eye on things, I daresay,' and she disappeared into the pavilion.

Her pleasure threatened to evaporate, but as soon as she got the boys into the little spinney at the edge of the field she cheered up again, pointing out various insects and helping them build a workable damn in the tiny stream that struggled down the ditch. They were getting horribly dirty, but hopefully Joy wouldn't be upset. Maybe she should offer to go home with them and bath them. Though actually the cricket ground was much closer to her own house – she could easily walk home from here. She was suddenly really glad she wasn't going to the pub afterwards. Was Joy going, she wondered. And if so, what about the boys? Did pubs allow children that young? She wasn't quite sure which pub they were going to, but if it was the Miners' Arms near here, then she knew there was a playground outside. Presumably if Joy sat outside the boys could play there. Would Clive sit outside with her? Or would Eric? Or would they all sit outside together? (And would Patrick wish she were there, too?)

She and the boys spent a happy hour or so until she saw that the match was just about over. Being careful to give them plenty of warning first, she disengaged them reasonably easily from the ditch and the three of them walked back to the pavilion.

'We're all going to the Miners' Arms, Ariel,' Joy met her at the steps, 'I know you aren't able to join us, but I could run you home first if you like.' Ellen had evidently phoned Joy during the week to explain about the restrictions – an action Ariel was now profoundly grateful for.

'Oh thanks, but actually I can easily walk from here.' Ariel knew that was the right response. 'See you next Saturday then. But not Sunday if it's an away match.'

'Next week's a home fixture, but you would see me anyway – I'm going to the away matches too. You could come with us if you like – me and Clive and Eric and Patrick. And the boys. It'll be a tight squeeze in the car but you're tiny. Unlike Eric, I have to say!' she laughed.

'I'm not sure. I won't be able to go to the pub afterwards, so I might have to catch the bus anyway.' Ariel struggled to keep her focus on what she knew were the important things and not start fantasising about Joy and Eric. Based on what, in any case?

'Bill Martin usually goes straight home after away matches. Even if Maisie comes with him, which she often doesn't. He could give you a lift home – I'll find out for you if you like.'

'That would be lovely. Thank you.' Ariel was relieved. 'Sorry the boys are so dirty…'

'Goodness that's all right. Sign they had a good time! Have a good week.'

•

'What are you reading?'

'The Great Gatsby'

'Why?' Pat always pronounced the word with two syllables and with an up-lilt at the end: 'Why-yuh?' She'd said that's how it was pronounced in Wales. 'And Glyn is Welsh, so I like to make him feel at home.'

'I think I'm going to take the summer course on English literature, so I'm giving my brain something serious to read for a change.'

'Is it any good?'

'It's supposed to be a classic. I have to say I'm not really into it though.' Ariel was disappointed. She didn't feel able to tell Pat that really she was reading it because Patrick had quoted from it, and she had been hoping to have what she thought of as Will-and-Ariel-like discussions with him about it. Paul had been pleased about it and had urged her to seriously consider the English Literature summer course, reminding her that at this point she needed to be taking a variety of courses to become well-rounded enough to gain a university place in less than a couple of years. Mr Woods had agreed, so telling herself they knew better about these things than she did, she had decided she would sign up this week.

'I wish you would come with me though.' She was not looking forward to beginning another new class without Pat. She'd thought that if Pat had been with her on the Ethics course she probably would never have dropped it.

'Not Pygmalion likely! I told you, I'm done with this lot, having nicely proved my point to the wasp-eating Miss Slimy-Socks. In any case, don't be so wet; you'll manage fine on your own, and probably make other friends – which god knows you need – as well.'

'I'm worried I won't see you again though,' Ariel voiced her real concern. 'I mean, we only really meet up because of P&L...'

'We're meeting now, aren't we? And we went Christmas shopping didn't we? And did the spa day. That's two Saturdays I gave up to be with you – my friend. And I put up with Glyn's moaning about never seeing me. So don't you start.'

'Sorry. And I do appreciate those Saturdays. But I do want to see you. I'll miss you.'

'I'll probably miss you, too. And when I do, I'll hop on the bus and meet you after class and we'll sink flesh-dissolving, industrial-strength, paint-stripping chemical chocolate drinks again and gossip just like the good old days.'

Ariel knew she had to be content with that. And tried not to think about the promised birthday present that had never materialised.

TWENTY-THREE

Saturday

Dear Will,

Where are you? I don't mean literally. I mean in my thoughts. Two years ago I used to have these wonderful conversations with you in my head and now several days – possibly even weeks – go by and you aren't there at all. Is that good? Or not? I wish you were here, so I could ask you. And again I realise how ridiculous that is because if you were here...well I won't say it again.

Instead I'll tell you that Pat would pronounce ridiculous as 'ridic-cull-ous' – not making the u a 'you' sound. She does that with other words, too. Ambulance, for example. And miraculous. I think it might be a Welsh thing, but whatever, it's fascinating to me. SHE is fascinating to me and I'm already missing her. Even though I've seen her this week for the last P&L class. I couldn't pin her down to when we'll meet again. She's probably right that I'll make other friends (well, maybe one...) in the literature class, but it won't be the same. I'm a one-friend person. As you'll know. When I had you I didn't want or need anyone else. And when I was seeing Pat three times a week I seem to have neglected you.

But in my own defence, there is Joy and her family (including her brother!) in my life, so I'm not totally friendless.

Yesterday I signed up for the literature class, which starts the week after next and is on Tuesdays and Thursdays from eleven to one. (I wish it could have been medieval literature, ala C S Lewis...). Pat said she'd come on the bus to find me but she's at school at those times. At least until the end of July. I mustn't be so 'wet', as she says. Anyway, that's not why I brought it up again. I found out that the book we are to read--- preferably before the class starts – is Franz Kafka's Metamorphosis. I only ordered it this morning so obviously haven't started it yet. But I already know from the description that it's about a young man who wakes up one morning as an insect of some sort. And I'm already feeling terribly sorry for him. I hope I enjoy it more than Gatsby – I don't 'get' that one at all. But perhaps I will after the literature class. Maybe that will open my eyes (or brain).

Time to go – tea at the Parkers and then my evening of babysitting. So this is the point I would normally write how much I miss you. I don't seem to want to write that tonight.

Which is actually fine because of course you aren't really there and you aren't really reading this. I think I used to pretend you were (both there, and reading this) because it helped. But I don't think it does any more. Actually, I seem – horrors! – not to be missing you so much. My life has changed SO much lately and so much of it is so good.

Not that my life with you WASN'T good, because it was. It was wonderful and I was more than broken-hearted when it ended. My life now is so very different.

Crikey, I think Mr Woods has actually had some influence on me and my thinking: it's not all black and white any more!

•

'How did you enjoy the cricket last week, Ariel?' Patrick had arrived almost as soon as the boys had gone to bed, as seemed to be his habit now.

'I had a great time, though I didn't see much of the actual match. Sorry you got out so quickly.'

'Yes. A bit rusty after the winter. A shame though, I was hoping to impress you with my batting skills.'

Ariel thought perhaps it had been unkind of her to mention it, so changed the subject. 'Have you read Metamorphosis by Franz Kafka?'

'I have, yes. A long time ago though. Why? Are you reading

it?'

'I will when it comes. I've only just ordered it.' She told him about signing up for the literature class.

'Good for you. I'm impressed. And rather envy you the experience of discovering all this for the first time. How did you get along with Nick Garroway and Jay Gatsby, by the way?'

'I didn't get it. I mean, I got the book, but I didn't get it, if you know what I mean. I couldn't see the point of it. The only bit I enjoyed was when Daisy asked about his house – as you'd quoted to me before.' She had not planned to be so blunt, but somehow couldn't make herself say things she didn't feel about the story. 'Sorry, I know it's a great classic. Hopefully I'll have learned how to appreciate "great classics" by the time I've finished the course.'

'What you should learn and what I hope you will learn is to have confidence in your own reactions. I love it that you are able to be so honest about it. And you know what – I didn't find it that great myself. As for the Kafka – well, I'll wait till you've read it before I comment.'

Ariel was thrilled. She would be having more meaningful conversations with Patrick. That was definitely something to look forward to. Life was indeed looking up.

She made them each a mug of tea and then, to her absolute delight, Patrick asked her if she'd like to work on the Times crossword puzzle with him. For a moment she was speechless, flooded with memories of doing it every day with Will and realising how much she had missed it. She had tried to continue by herself but it had caused her more pain than pleasure, even as she arrived at the correct answers.

'We've done well!' he was impressed. 'We should do this every week, methinks.'

'I'd like that,' she said as calmly as she could, whilst thinking to herself every week! He's coming every week! 'I used to do this with, with the man I sort of told you about. Or no, I haven't actually, have I?' She was flustered now, but he either didn't notice or had decided not to.

'Shall I tell you my all-time favourite clue? It was simply the letters G S G E: two words, nine and four.'

She thought for a minute, then 'Eggs, maybe?…for the four… but…oh! scrambled eggs! Wonderful!'

'And so are you! You've obviously got the right sort of quirky brain for this stuff.'

She knew she blushed as she hugged the word 'quirky' to herself. She liked being thought quirky, especially because for Patrick it was obviously an admirable quality. Surely, she thought, surely this week he'll offer to take me home. But he didn't. When the Parkers returned he began talking to Joy about their father's impending visit, and neither of them did more than wave a casual 'bye, see you tomorrow,' as she and Clive left the house for him to drive her home.

•

Sunday's cricket match followed pretty much the same pattern as the week before, except that Patrick scored a more respectable 31 and it was Eric's turn to be out for a duck first ball. Ariel noticed that Patrick did not tease Eric about it. She also noticed that Joy managed several times to be within touching distance of Eric at the tea table, leaning over him as she refilled his mug, briefly rubbing his back as she passed with a plate of sliced nut bread. Clive, on the far side of the table and about as far away from Eric as possible, was deep in conversation with Derek and the captain of the opposing team. She wondered if he'd done that deliberately, so as not to be near Eric and therefore forced to be aware of what was happening.

The visiting team had batted first, so Joy had opted for making sandwiches whilst Ariel played Snap and Ludo with Graham and Nigel on the veranda of the pavilion. From this position she'd been happy to see Patrick take a difficult catch and was pleased with herself when she'd successfully got the little boys to clap and cheer.

Immediately after tea Patrick sought her out to introduce her to Brenda, the scorer, who suggested she might benefit from sitting with her for a while to see the scoring actually being recorded.

'I'll just check with Joy about the boys,' Ariel began, remembering why she was there.

'They'll be fine,' Brenda reassured her. 'Their dad looks after them when he's not actually at the wicket – which isn't a lot, as you'll see. I think his record is something like four balls. But he's a good bowler.'

Ariel tried to absorb that and not think about what it might mean that Clive looked after Graham and Nigel, rather than Joy, but knew she had to set it aside for now whilst she concentrated on the scoring. As Patrick had given her a detailed lesson a few weeks ago, she knew exactly what to do and was pleased when Brenda passed her the book and said 'here, you do it for a few overs and see how you get on.'

Brenda watched her closely for a while, then, 'You've got it. I'm here if you need me, but I think you know what you're doing. Check with him,' nodding toward the visiting scorer who had been introduced as Philip, 'at the end of every over to make sure you're in sync.'

'And if we're not,' said Philip, 'we toss up for who changes their record.'

'We Do Not,' Brenda frowned. 'These things have to be spot-on accurate. People get very funny about their statistics you know.'

Philip winked at Ariel who quickly suppressed her grin and concentrated on the scorer's book. Nothing untoward happened and she was both relieved and sorry when the match was over and the three of them compared their two books.

'You coming down the pub, Bren?' Philip asked.

'No I am not. I don't drink, as you well know. No, I'm going to church to pray for drunken sots like you lot.' She snapped the book shut and stood up. 'Should I give the book to you, Ariel, or shall I let Arthur take care of it?

'Oh, I don't know…' Ariel hadn't thought about this. What if for some reason she couldn't go to the away match and she had the book. She began to feel anxious.

'I'll give it to Arthur then. Nice to meet you. See you in a couple of weeks I expect.'

'Bye gorgeous,' Philip called after her, winking at Ariel again. 'Phew, she's hard-going that one. Absolutely nothing in the way of a sense of humour. I shall be glad to see you when your lot come to us next month. You coming for a quick one?'

'No, afraid not, but not because I'm going to church,' Ariel was pleased with her own casualness. 'Nice to meet you, too and I'll see you again when we come to you.'

She couldn't see Joy (or Eric) but said goodbye to Clive and the boys and set off to walk home. Good day? On the whole, yes, she thought. Janet, Maisie and Alice had welcomed her back and the team had all nodded happily at her at tea time. None of them teased her in quite the same way they teased Maisie, who, at 18 was closest to her age, but then they probably didn't feel they knew her well enough yet. And she had really enjoyed doing the scoring. She had warmed to Brenda as well as to Philip, though in different ways. And there was something about entering the information after each ball that was enormously satisfying, even comforting, to her. It helped her not think too much about Joy, for one thing. And about Eric, for another.

Yes. A good day. With the prospect of many more like it, she hoped.

•

'Hopefully you've all ready Metamorphosis. If you haven't, then please do so by next session or you will be seriously out of touch with what's happening in this class.'

Ariel cautiously looked around to see how the other students were reacting to this rather abrupt start to the class. Those she could see from her seat on the side aisle were simply looking, mostly expressionless, at the instructor who couldn't, she thought, be more different from the affable Mr Woods. For one

137

thing, she was female: Mrs Barrett, she had written on the chalkboard, right below English Literature 501X.

'Franz Kafka was born in Prague in 1883 where his parents had a fancy goods store. He had three sisters, all of whom were to die in the gas chambers. That alone should give you an insight into the crushing guilt that pervades all of Kafka's work and is where we'll start when we begin discussing Metamorphosis...'

Mrs Barrett droned on and on, hardly pausing for breath. Ariel frantically tried to write down all she was saying but was very aware she was missing large chunks of the narrative. Another part of her brain was conscious of how very different this class was from P&L and how, so far, she wasn't liking it at all. She didn't like the book, she didn't like the lecturer and she didn't like the way the session was going. But she couldn't give up, she couldn't have another failure. She'd vowed that withdrawing from the Ethics class would be her first and last such negative experience.

There was a ten-minute break at noon, when Mrs Barrett and most of the students went outside for a quick smoke or down the corridor to the toilets. Ariel stayed at her desk and read over what she'd written, hoping it would make sense later; it certainly didn't now.

'Flippin' 'eck – she's givin' me writer's cramp.' A boy two rows in front of Ariel turned round and smiled ruefully at her.

'Me too – are you getting it all down?'

'Trying to. Thing is, though, you don't know what's important yet. We might be wasting our energy when all we need to be doing is listening to her. She hasn't said we have to take notes, you'll notice.'

'Oh.' Ariel hadn't thought of that. 'Shall we ask her?'

'You can if you like. I ain't putting my head over the garden wall this early on. She has a reputation for eating students alive you know. You have to admit, she looks as if she snaps the tops off beer bottles with her teeth. Not that she'd probably get within three miles of a beer bottle. Might help her if she did. God 'elp Mr Barrett, if there is one. I shouldn't like to wake up next to her every day.'

Ariel had been hoping he would offer to ask; she knew she wasn't going to, even before he'd warned her about Mrs Barrett's fearsome reputation. She spared a thought for the hapless Mr Barrett.

The second half of the session was just like the first. When there was less than five minutes to go, Mrs Barrett paused her narrative, took a deep breath and said, 'Alienation and guiltless guilt'. She scrawled it on the chalkboard. 'Write a few paragraphs about how they are demonstrated in at least one place in the book and if you haven't read the whole of it yet, DO SO. Dismissed.'

Ariel wondered if she should walk out with the boy who had spoken to her at the break, but saw immediately that he left quickly with a small group of other students. She packed up her notebook and pen, and got up to leave. She was aware of a huge emptiness inside and of missing Pat. This moment, the end of class and chatting with Pat in and outside the cafeteria, had been some of the best times of her experience last term. She walked out slowly, pausing to look in the cafeteria just in case Pat had somehow materialised there (of course she hadn't) and then out to the bus stop. She ought to have brought some lunch – should she go back to the cafeteria and get something? She didn't want to; she didn't want to sit there alone. Not that sitting alone in and of itself would trouble her, but sitting there without Pat, after class, would only increase her sense of loneliness. No, she'd go home and get something to eat there and then start on the assignment.

Pat would have asked if they needed to take notes. And Pat would have made her giggle about what the boy had said about waking up next to Mrs Barrett. Would Pat have said something was a trick question, too? If so, what? Something about the 'guiltless guilt' perhaps?

'For heaven's sake don't be so wet!' she scolded herself as she got off the bus and began the short walk up their road. She couldn't go through life stuck to Pat like a Siamese twin – who you weren't supposed to call that any more. They were conjoined twins now. She'd better start getting used to being on her own and then she might find a friend or two in the class.

Or she might not. And even if she did, a new friend would not replace Pat.

TWENTY-FOUR

Saturday

I should have listened to the Pat in my head! There WAS a 'trick question'. Not the bit about guiltless guilt, but the taking notes bit. On Thursday Dragon Lady said 'one or two of you have complained that you're finding it hard to take notes because I'm talking so much. Have I asked you to take notes? I have not. Fact sheets will be issued each week that will contain everything I have said on both Tuesdays and Thursdays.' Why didn't I realise she was reading from her notes, and why oh why couldn't she have said that at the start of the first class? Because she's a sadist, Pat would said. (I love how I'm channelling Pat now. It's nearly as good as having her here. No it isn't.)

Anyway. That makes college life so much better. I can sit and listen – and wonder who had the nerve to ask her about note-taking – and really absorb what she says instead of panicking that I haven't got everything down on paper. Still not quite trusting her though, so I jot down things I definitely want to remember – that's only sensible, I think. She hasn't said what we'll need to do to pass the course yet. Nobody dares ask her if there will be an exam or a written take-home paper, so I'm trying to be ready for either. Or even both.

Now that I've read Metamorphosis (twice, actually) I'm looking forward to seeing Patrick tonight and having a good discussion with him about it.

If he comes.

•

'Are Kafka and his wretched Gregor Samsa holding your interest better than Fitzgerald's so-called pièce de résistance?'

Ariel had made them both tea and was more than ready to talk about her literature class. 'Well, yes and no. It's certainly having an impact on me; I can't stop thinking about the poor lad, whereas I can't say I had any feelings for any of the characters in Gatsby. Except perhaps irritation.'

'With them or with yourself?'

'Oh.' Ariel pondered. 'Both, I suppose. But it worries me that I don't see the point of either story actually. I think Mrs Barrett is trying to get us to understand why Metamorphosis was written. She's a fierce and frightening dragon lady, by the way. The whole class is terrified of her.'

'Ah yes, I know who she is and while it would give me great pleasure to tell you she is a pussy cat in real life, the truth is, she's a horror!' Patrick chuckled. 'I've done some work for her husband – he's Dr Barrett the dentist in Gosforth, you know, and he's just about as difficult as she is reputed to be.'

'That's comforting. I hope I'm never in need of his services. No wonder she's chosen Kafka for us then. It must warm her inner sadist.'

'Ooh, you really don't like her, do you? I've never known you be anything other than positive about people. Good to know there's a bit of hate in you too.'

'Oh no, not hate! I can heartily dislike her, but I can't hate her. I decided not to hate anyone, after I read the agony aunt column in one of Joy's magazines. She points out that hate is just as close a bond as love, keeping you attached to the person you hate in the same way love does. I know this sounds pious, but I think it's probably better to cultivate indifference.' Ariel hoped she didn't sound too sickeningly saintly. She'd read the article at a time when Pat was apparently urging her to switch from loving Will to hating him, so the idea that this would bind her to Will in a similar way had troubled her. Not that she could ever imagine being indifferent to Will, but it was a start. She could never have expressed this opinion to Pat, but on the whole she thought Patrick would be all right with it.

'You're very wise. I shall try to adopt your attitude; it's much healthier.'

She looked closely at him to see if he was mocking her, but he seemed sincere enough.

'You should think about studying psychology, Ariel. I think you'd find it fascinating. It might even help you make sense of why, in the story, Père Samsa's reaction to his monstrous insect son was so brutal.'

'I really didn't like that bit – I found it so upsetting that his own father could be so vile. I almost couldn't read on from there. I cried at the idea of him struggling to the door with the apple his father had thrown at him stuck in his back. It's so horrible.'

'Can't imagine your father reacting like that, can you?'

Ariel felt a huge wave of sadness all over her body, beginning at her toes and working its way up to the top of her head. She knew Patrick was referring to Howard (and he was probably right; Howard would have been much kinder than Gregor's father) but it was Will as her father who was filling her mind with tender and empathic images and memories. Mr Samsa was more like Jock, her abusive and often cruel stepfather. The wave receded and she became aware that Patrick was still speaking.

'When he was in his thirties Franz apparently wrote a 45-page letter—forty-five pages!— to his father, listing all the reasons he loathed and despised him. It's worth reading, that letter, because some of the things on the list are so trivial you want to shake the bloke and say "get a grip, man!" He even admits, in that letter, that his dad was basically kind-hearted and tender, but rants at considerable length about his pig-at-the-trough eating habits and his propensity for telling off-colour jokes. It all sounds fairly typical teenage angst to me, so I'm not sure really that Kafka's own father's behaviour does entirely justify the portrayal of Gregor's father.'

'Fathers are very sensitive subjects with me, actually. I didn't know my own father until recently when I came to live with him. I had a horrible stepfather and he was the reason I ran away from home and ended up with a man I thought could be my father. The only trouble was, it wasn't a daughter he was looking for.' She looked at Patrick to gauge his reaction. It seemed all right, so she continued. 'He was grooming me – I've only just realised that, only just learned the word in that connection, actually – to be his wife when I was sixteen. Or before, if he could have got away with it. He had this obsession with Will and Ariel Durant and we were not only to continue their philosophical work, but actually become them, apparently. I went along with it because he was mostly wonderful to me. I'm only just realising how much he was working to his own agenda and not doing anything other than paying lip service to mine. Which was to be his daughter, of course. He hated that idea and was furious with me when he found out I'd told the postman he was my Dad.' She stopped, suddenly wondering where in the world she was going with this saga, and what on earth Patrick was making of it. 'Anyway. That's why I'm on the At Risk Register I suppose. He'd abducted me. In case you're wondering. It's not because I've actually murdered anyone.' She tried for a smile but failed miserably.

'I never had you down as a murderer, Ariel.' Patrick smiled gently. 'And thank you for telling me this. It can't have been easy for you and it must be nearly intolerable for you to read about Samsa's cruelty to his son. If I can help... even if it's just someone to listen and possibly help keep you on track with the course...'

Despite herself, Ariel shrugged. She also tried to smile her thanks. 'Well, let's have some more tea then – at least I will. Do you want some cider?'

Patrick nodded, looking solemn, and she disappeared into the kitchen to make her tea and get his cider. She was reluctant to return to the lounge, not knowing how to move the conversation on, yet knowing she'd had enough of talking about Metamorphosis and herself and Will.

She needn't have worried. Patrick accepted his cider with thanks and rapidly launched into plans for getting her to the away match tomorrow. She took her cue from him and responded immediately. It was quickly settled that she would come here to the Parkers on the bus for half past twelve and the seven of them – four Parkers, Patrick, Eric and herself – would drive to Snettingham in time for the two o'clock start. Bill Martin would drive her home. Patrick was complimentary about her scoring last week and they talked about cricket until, somehow, the mood lightened.

For a change, she hoped he wouldn't offer to take her home, and was mostly relieved when he didn't.

•

'This is my third week – fifth actual class session – in English Lit without Pat,' she scolded herself as she waited for Mrs Barrett to appear. 'And I still don't know a soul in this room.' She turned to the girl sitting across the aisle. "My name's Ariel, what's yours?'

The girl looked blankly at her for a few seconds. Then, flatly, 'Karina,' and she turned back to the magazine she was reading.

Ariel mentally shrugged. Well, she'd tried. She'd try again, with someone else, next class. She looked around the classroom. There were, she counted, eighteen students not including herself. Okay, she'd had no luck with one, so that left seventeen. If she introduced herself to one every class it would take eight weeks after this week. Not enough time left. And anyway, she knew she wouldn't be able to take more than one more rejection. Maybe not even that. She felt worse for trying, missing Pat even more, remembering how easy it had been to connect with her, and haranguing herself for being so needy.

Mrs Barrett had begun asking for input from the students last Thursday, but the discussions had been tentative, halting, to say the least. Today she asked of no one in particular what they thought of Kafka's on-off engagement with Felice Bauer. When it became clear no one had anything to say – or, in Ariel's case, at least, the courage to say it – she added, 'You will remember that he ended the engagement initially in 1914, then renewed it for a few months in 1916, only to abruptly terminate it permanently. It has been suggested that fear of sex or of impotence was the motivation for these reversals. However, Kafka himself stated that his goal for himself and any partner was the pursuit of a path to spiritual perfection, which required strict self-control. Any comments?' There were none, and she continued, 'Of course it could also be that the not-very-lovely Felice had a habit of loudly crunching sugar lumps, rather like a horse.' She laughed and snorted at the same time, but only one or two students reacted with a smile. 'Yes?'

Again nobody spoke up. Ariel felt herself getting hot, wanting to ask questions, anxious to hear more about this, but could not bring herself to speak. Would Will have said they, she and him, were 'pursuing a path of spiritual perfection'? She rather thought he would, even though he had never said anything like that as far as she could remember. She wasn't even quite sure what it meant actually.

'All right. If you can't or won't speak about it, then please write about it for the next session. I will choose someone – randomly and arbitrarily – to read out their offering. Dismissed.'

'Oh god, don't let it be me,' Ariel sent up a heartfelt prayer. Glancing around she guessed that most, if not all, the others were doing the same. She wondered how many students would simply not show up on Thursday. Maybe she wouldn't either. She wouldn't decide now; she'd see what she could write first and then make up her mind.

She walked out with Karina who seemed oblivious to their earlier mutual introduction, and who said and did nothing to indicate she was even aware of Ariel's presence next to her. Ariel sighed and turned off into the toilet where she waited for a few minutes, giving her classmates time to disappear. 'It shouldn't be this way,' she said to herself sadly, as she walked to the bus stop where she was just in time to see her bus pulling away.

At this time of day buses were fairly frequent so she decided to wait there, rather than repairing to the cafeteria. And was glad she did, for the next bus to pull up, on the opposite side of the road, was the number 32 and to her utter delight, off got Pat.

'Crikey! Oh I am SO pleased to see you. Why are you here though?' Ariel couldn't believe her eyes.

'Why am I here? To see you, you ninny. Why do you think I'm here?' Pat hugged her hard. 'Hot choccy?'

'Oh please! I'm so glad to see you I'll even buy you a cake to go with it. Two cakes, if you want.'

They got their drinks and cakes and took them to their usual spot under the tree outside the cafeteria.

'Are you bunking off school?' Ariel was concerned despite her happiness at seeing her friend so unexpectedly.

'No, we broke up last week. I'm a free agent at last. I'm not invited back, either, which suits me just fine. My mother says I have to get a job but I shall take my time looking for one. I haven't been a prisoner at school all these years just to swap their jail cells for another one quite yet. No, I'm having my summer holiday first, thank you.'

'I thought you were going to be working for Glyn.' Ariel hoped nothing had gone wrong with their plans.

'I am, but there's not really enough to do yet. His Dad gives him some work and he – the Dad – can probably find a slot for me in their office when I'm ready. I'm not wildly excited about it, but I can doubtless make my own hours to a certain extent. At any rate, it'll be better than rounding up rogue trollies at the supermarket. How's life with you? How's the luscious Patrick – kissed you yet?'

Ariel laughed. 'Of course not.'

'What do you mean, "of course not"? Why the hell not? Is he gay?' Pat glared indignantly at her.

'I'd never thought about it.' Ariel tried not to feel shocked at Pat's question. 'How do you tell if someone's gay?'

'Well they might tell you. Or they might be so camp you can't help but notice. Or they might never attempt to kiss an attractive girl they spend every Saturday evening with. No, Ariel, I'm mostly joking. I think. But you seem to be considering it as a serious possibility.'

'I don't know that I am. I honestly hadn't ever thought about it. You'd ask him, I suppose, but I can't.'

'Nope, not even I would be that crass. But you're still seeing him? Going to the cricket and all? How's that going? And how's the head-trip class going – made a ton of friends there?'

Ariel answered the questions as best she could, doing her best to put a positive yet realistic spin on it all, but inside feeling upset by Pat's question about Patrick as well as struggling not to talk about Joy and Eric. She'd wanted to tell Pat that Patrick had commented on her 'quirky' brain, but realised without saying anything that Pat would not think that was good. Or cool.

'Have you replaced me as Best Friend yet?' Pat smiled as she said it, but Ariel suddenly knew she would have minded very much if the answer had been yes. It was an uncharacteristically tight smile for Pat.

'Never. Haven't really talked with any one much and certainly nobody I could say is a friend. I told you, you're irreplaceable.' She reached over and squeezed Pat's hand as she spoke.

'Too right. That's what Glyn says, too. I must be doing something right.' Pat lay back on the grass and looked up at the sky. 'Hello up there, God. Hope You're having a good day. Do you believe in God, Ariel?'

'I don't know. I really want to. I would love to be able to just pray to some almighty power and feel He would take care of everything for me. Do you?'

'I think I must do. You know I prayed when I thought I was up the duff. Glyn believes – he got converted in prison, he says. He even wants us to start going to church but I'm not sure I'm ready to go that far.'

'Will – you know, that man – he was adamant there was no god, so for a long time I accepted his word. But after he died I wanted so much to believe he'd gone to heaven, or somewhere where he could keep watch over me. And where I would eventually join him. I even used to write my journal like a letter to him. I think it's the afterlife bit I most want to believe in. It's hard to know I'll never see Will again.' She paused for a moment and pondered. 'At least, it used to be hard. I'm not so sure now.' She was silent for a few minutes, and felt relieved that Pat was too. 'Sometimes I feel so angry with him…'

'That could be because he's left you. Or it could be because you see him more clearly, do you think?'

'Maybe both,' Ariel shrugged. 'Tell you what though, when I first met you I wrote to Will in my journal to tell him how wise you were. And I hardly even knew you then, but I somehow saw that about you.'

'Oh bloody hell! You need a bit more fun in your life, Ariel. What say we do something after your Thursday class? Just you and me. I've missed your adulation, my little friend.'

'I never thought it would be possible to embarrass you, Pat. You're almost blushing! But you are wise, and YES, whatever you'd like, I'm up for it. Class ends at one, so we could start with lunch if you like.'

'Not here though. Their food is lethal. Let's take a picnic somewhere picturesque? And you can tell me more about you and Will and your amazing life before I met you. You fascinate me, you know. And don't think I've forgotten about your birthday present. It's taking me longer than I thought, but you'll have it. I promise.'

'Thanks, I'm looking forward to it.' Happiness surged through her again.

'Hm. You might actually not like it at all,' Pat shook her head. 'You might even hate it. And actually, you might hate me, too.'

TWENTY-FIVE

Saturday

So much to think about from my times this week with Pat, not to mention my 'confession' to Patrick and his reaction.

Perhaps I could be accused of being trivial, but I'm most intrigued by Pat's mention of my much-delayed birthday present. I had almost given up thinking about that. Surely she doesn't feel she has to keep mentioning it and yet will actually never produce it. She's much too honest for that, I'm sure. But why did she say I might hate it? Or even hate her? I'm sure I shan't. I know I was disappointed by her Christmas present, but the mere fact that she is getting me something means so much. 'It's not the gift, it's the thought that counts' after all, and nothing can spoil my joy that I was on her Christmas list with her parents and her boyfriend. And nobody else! I was special.

Patrick was so lovely when we talked about Gregor Samsa's horrible father and my reaction to it. But IS he gay? If he is, why would he come to Joy's every Saturday night to be with me? Because that's safe, Pat said. Is that the image I project? I don't think Ivor thought I was 'safe' in that way, though he probably ended up thinking I was frigid. Perhaps I am.

Pat asked me if I'm turned on by Patrick. I couldn't answer. I know I like him, and I know I feel comfortable, mostly, with him, but honestly I don't have that funny feeling in my innards like I did sometimes when I was with Will. I think that's what Pat means by 'turned on'. But does that mean something about Patrick or about me?

Do I want him to kiss me? I do, because that would mean he wants to be 'that way' with me. But I don't, because I don't have that quivery feeling in my belly etc. when I think about it. Perhaps that would come though, if he did kiss me.

Actually, I think the basis of my liking him is because he is similar to Will in so many good ways: his mind/intelligence, his pleasure in discussing things and the way he talks about things,

150

his... his... what? I'm stuck for the right words here. The word (non-word, actually) unthreateningness keeps hammering at the door to my mind, yet I'm pretty sure I never felt that way about Will. I didn't feel threatened by him exactly, but I do feel, now, that a certain ominousness was never very far away. (Another non-word?) And yet I loved him, utterly, completely, in a thought-I-would-die-without-him, sort of way.

Oh well, all this is keeping me from dwelling on Joy and her all-too-obvious flirtation with Eric. Driving to the away matches is painful. The boys sit in their booster seats in the far back, Clive drives, Patrick sits in the front with him, and I sit wedged by the window in the back, trying to take up as little space as possible, with two rather plump bodies crushed up against each other beside me. SURELY it would make more sense for one of them to sit in the front – Joy, for example. She's Clive's WIFE for heaven's sake. Thankfully Bill drives me home, with or without Maisie, whom I really like. We had a giggle at the last match and I felt a real bond with her. It started over something Janet had said to Arthur and then she scolded Maisie for smiling at him because she was annoyed with him. It was all very trivial, but somehow M and I bonded over it and she said last Sunday she'd come to more away fixtures now I was coming, even though I'd be busy with the scoring.

That's TWO people who seek out my company. No, three now: Maisie, Patrick and Pat. And really you could count Graham and Nigel if they had the power to seek me out on their own. They certainly adore me.

Pat and I are going to get together every Thursday after my class for the next few weeks (until her mother prevails and Pat has to get a job.)

Why would Pat think I might hate her over the birthday present? I don't 'do' hate.

●

'Why did you ask me if I believe in God, Pat?' They were

having lunch at Pat's house. Ariel had caught the bus there at her friend's request. She'd asked if she should bring anything but Pat had already been out and got them both fish and chips which they were now drenching in sea salt and vinegar and noisily enjoying as they sat on the deck outside the kitchen.

'It worries me that you only have me to turn to.'

'No, seriously.'

'I am serious.' Pat put her fork down. 'If anything happened between us, who would give you comfort and support? I know you've been through hell and survived, but you sometimes strike me as quite fragile. And anyway, as well, I'm coming round to Glyn's way of thinking: that everyone needs what he calls a Higher Power to keep them on the straight and narrow, and in your case, to look after you emotionally. Oh don't worry – I'm not going to be all pious and saintly. Glyn isn't like that anyway. He's the strong and silent type when it comes to his feelings – except about me, of course; he can wax pretty lyrical about how he feels about me. No, he uses his HP like a sort of conscience to keep him being good. You know, they say prison doesn't work, but it has certainly changed my lovely Glyn.'

'What was he like before then?' Ariel was fascinated – and keen to avoid discussing her fragility with Pat.

'UN-godly as hell. Drank too much, not always honest, and not the happy man he is now. He reckons it's my influence, standing by him and all that, but I think his chats with the prison chaplain had a huge effect on him too. And actually I like him better now I've got used to it.'

'Do you think you'll get married one day? To him, I mean.'

'Probably. And of course him. But not for years – I'm only seventeen, I don't want to commit to anything more permanent than we already have until I'm at least twenty. Much to my mother's relief, I have to say.' Pat began clearing up the wrappers and plates. 'Sit still, I'll make us some coffee and then you can tell me something scintillating about you and Will. I'm in a mood to be shocked, so make it juicy please.'

Ariel pondered. What could she tell Pat that would shock her, she wondered. She'd never told anyone the exact details of her abduction; in truth, she could hardly remember it herself. In her memory, she had met Will when she was running away from home in Sheringham, on her way to Norwich where she'd thought her real father lived, and she had gone willingly with him to his house in the Midlands. Why had she done that? And what had happened next? Had she struggled to get away? Had she wanted to get away? She surely wouldn't have wanted to go back to Sheringham, and Jock, but why had she given up her plan to find her birth father? Her memories of the time with Will were so lovely for the most part that it was hard to think she had ever not wanted to be there.

He had introduced her to cryptic crosswords, killer Sudoku, music, poetry, literature, cricket, tennis, bird watching, and deep, philosophical and logical thinking. He had improved her grammar and her vocabulary immeasurably. He had taught her to cook and together they had learned to skate. She had learned how to be in the world by observing him (just as she was re-learning now, by watching, and emulating whenever possible, Pat, and sometimes, lately, Ellen). She had loved being his pupil and had eagerly sopped up everything he had tried to teach her, even some fairly obtuse ideas and beliefs that she'd hardly understood from Walt Whitman and of course from his heroes, Will and Ariel Durant. They had spent all day, every day, together, doing things for fun, or housework or working on their 'project' together. For the last few months they had even spent their nights together, sleeping in the same bed, cuddling for most of the night.

Would that be shocking to Pat? Probably not as much as the fact that they had only cuddled. Pat had not gone into detail, but Ariel had a feeling that she and Glyn had been sexually active for three years or more and quite possibly there had been other sexual partners before Glyn. And maybe even as well as Glyn, in their early days. Mind you, Ariel had only been ten (as she'd thought) when she had first met Will. She had actually been eleven, and had had a birthday, thus making her twelve, about a month later. She had been almost fourteen when Will was killed and, had not that disaster happened, planning to make love with him that very night. They'd had a sort of pact that she could kiss him on the lips when she was fourteen, emulating her namesake

Ariel's behaviour with her then teacher, Will Durant. She hadn't waited though. She had impulsively kissed him as provocatively as she knew how, resulting in their decision to consummate their love sexually that night. And not so incidentally, resulting in Will's careless driving and subsequent fatal car crash.

Would that shock Pat? Or should she tell her about her cruel stepfather, Jock, who had not only--on countless occasions-- pulled her knickers off and thrashed her with his belt, but also, often, would feel around her genitals afterwards, poking his filthy fingers inside her and leering at her with his foul-smelling face pressed hard against her wet-with-tears cheeks. Afterwards she'd scrub her face to get rid of the smell of him, and sit in the bath to wash off the stickiness that somehow seemed to be on her legs. She didn't think she'd wet herself, but at the time had thought that perhaps in her distress that's what had happened and she hadn't realised. She knew now that she had not.

Will had never hit her. He'd hardly ever shouted at her, or even been mildly cross. Except on that awful morning when he'd discovered she'd been talking to the postman and telling him that Will was her Dad. Oh how she had wanted him to be her Dad. Not her lover, but because he was so lovely to her, she was willing to do almost anything he'd asked out of gratitude. And yet, in Pat's terms, she'd fancied him too. She knew she did. Even at the time she knew she did.

And now he was dead. And Jock was in prison. And her mother never made contact with her or responded on the rare occasions Ariel had sent a card – usually out of guilt. And now she was living with her real dad, Howard, who was turning out to be all right really, and her stepmother, Ellen, whom she had come to like, even love, very much.

•

'Sorry for the delay. I was looking for the whiskey.' Pat returned with mugs of coffee.

'Whiskey?' Ariel couldn't keep the astonishment out of her voice. 'What do you want whiskey for?'

'Glyn's godmother is Scottish and he told me that when he visited her up there when he was a little lad, she'd often have the local vicar person round. Only he wasn't called a vicar, it was something else, but never mind. Anyway, she'd brew up a pot of tea and say "and whill you be having a whee cinder in your tea, meenister?" Glyn says it in a lovely lilting Scottish burr. Turns out the "cinder" was a hefty slug of whiskey and naturally the good minister always said "whell, aye, and why not?" So I thought we might give it a go too, but I couldn't find any whiskey. There's a bottle of cooking sherry but I already know that's foul, so we'll do without.'

'Well I can't say I'm not glad!' Ariel drank her coffee with relief that it was only coffee.

'Yeah. Probably a bad idea. I have a lot of bad ideas, you know. But I'm lovely with it.' Pat tucked her legs beneath her and turned her chair towards Ariel. 'So give! Tell me more about Himself.'

'I was thinking while you were inside that I really don't know very much about him at all. I suppose he was what you'd call secretive about his past. Sometimes, in the beginning, I'd ask questions and he never really gave me any answers and often got quite offish – which stopped me asking pretty quickly.'

'But if you lived in his house, you must have seen evidence of his life – photos of his family, for instance.'

'No. He said his parents were both dead, but they'd left him enough money so he didn't have to work. I think he had it invested and he did things with it on the computer, but he never showed me any of that.'

'No brothers and sisters? No ex-wife?'

'No. He did mention a cousin who'd evidently been to stay with him, but she'd died, too, he said. I think he'd said her name was Sally and she'd left a lot of her clothes and things in boxes in a cupboard in my bedroom.' Ariel struggled to remember accurately. 'He gave a lot of them to me when I needed some new things. Even some sanitary pads. '

'Jesus! Sounds very mysterious to me. Why would she leave

her things there – unless she visited a lot, but then when she died wouldn't he send all her things back to her own home? Or dump them on the local charity shop?'

'I hadn't thought about it. I do remember wondering why the boxes were marked A-I and A-II, not Sally something, but I never asked him about it. I did ask him what she died of and he got a bit irritated with me, so I backed off straight away.'

Pat looked thoughtful. 'I looked up Will Dee on the internet the other day when I had nothing better to do.'

'Pat!' Ariel was shocked.

'Don't worry. I didn't discover anything. The only Will Dee I found was something called a player spoof in RuneScape. He's only found in the "evolution of combat" apparently, whatever that means. I'm not a RuneScape aficionado and I'll bet you're not either.'

'No I am not. I have no idea what you're even talking about.' She hoped she didn't sound too frosty. She desperately didn't want them to fall out.

They sat in silence for a few moments. Ariel really wanted to leave but felt she couldn't without making a scene, even if she simply said goodbye. She practised in her head. 'Well, time for me to be going. See you next Thursday?' It wouldn't sound casual, she knew it wouldn't.

Pat eventually broke the silence. 'How's your lit class? I hear Mrs Barrett is a right ptarmigan.'

Ariel couldn't help laughing. 'You mean termagant! A ptarmigan is a bird. Like a pheasant or a partridge, that sort of thing. But yes, you've heard right – she can be very tart, not at all encouraging like Mr Woods. She terrifies me.'

'Whatever. I made you laugh though. And I'll bet you keep your head well down and then turn in exquisitely written assignments. Are you getting all As?'

'So far. But it hasn't always been easy. I sort of like it and I sort of don't. I'll be glad when it's over but Paul says hardly any instructors are as pleasant as Mr Woods and I should get used to what life is really like.'

'Hm, he's probably right, but then, why should we? Why shouldn't we have the lovely things and leave the unlovely to the masochists? Mind you, your mate C S Lewis says hardship prepares an ordinary person for an extraordinary destiny. So rock on, Ariel, it's looking good for you, I'd say. Are you still having Paul then?

'Not for the summer. He'll be back in September but he says he sees his role coming to an end and that I should be taking more and more at the college so I can apply for a university place at the earliest date. If I want to go, that is. I'm not really sure yet. I think I probably will though. Want to, that is.' This was much safer ground. Ariel began to relax and open up again, happy to mull over possibilities with her friend. 'I have no idea what I want to do though. I envy you there.'

They continued chatting for another hour or so, until Ariel felt able to say her practised goodbye in a normal tone. Pat waited with her at the bus stop, giving her a quick but full of meaning hug as the bus appeared. 'I'm really enjoying our girlie Thursdays – see you next week, little friend. And "don't forget to love yourself" – that's a quote from Kierkegaard, you know. Never assume I didn't learn a little something from my one and only college class.'

TWENTY-SIX

Saturday

Brought my journal to the Parkers again because I knew I was going to be alone: Joy's father is visiting and Patrick arrived right after tea and now they are all out for dinner at some posh restaurant in Newcastle to celebrate Mr Cavendish's birthday.

He's quite sweet. I don't think he remembered me – after all, we met very briefly in London and he was busy sorting out the tickets for us – but he asked all the sort of questions that grownups seem to like to ask and then didn't listen to the answers! He is obviously quite smitten with his grandsons though and seemed pleased that I feel the same way.

It's been so long that I was here alone that I'm a bit lost for something to do.

Looking back through my journal I'm struck by how much and how quickly I seem to change my mind about things. The name change, for example. I haven't thought about that for weeks. So thinking about it now, I know I'm going to stay Ariel. And hope that one day Howard and Ellen might manage to think of me that way. I think they'd probably call me Ariel if I asked them to, but I want them to think of me as Ariel too, because that's how I think of myself. I suppose the first step towards that would be for me to ask them to start calling me by that name. I'll test the waters with Ellen, and see what she thinks Howard might say.

Do I want to be Dee or Pike? I've even thought about Pyke because it looks more esoteric. (Or do I mean exotic?) But it sounds the same, so what would be the point? I seem to have decided to keep Jessica as a middle name. Ariel Jessica Pike. Ariel Jessica Dee. Ariel Jessica Cavendish?

•

Sunday night and sleep wouldn't come. And trying to find comfort in the thought that nothing had changed, only her awareness of it, simply wasn't working. Because, actually, for a change, something had changed.

She'd managed to act fairly normally at the match – nothing could interfere with her scoring duties – and coming home with Bill and Maisie because it had started to rain just as the match ended, she had not even allowed her shock at what she'd heard to affect her. She hoped. She would not have liked either of them to think it mattered to her if Patrick was gay. Because actually, it didn't. It didn't matter one iota, she told herself again, as she turned over for the umpteenth time and waited, again in vain, for sleep.

It had begun at teatime; the conversation had been around whether or not the tea ladies could round up enough players to stage a challenge match against the men. Janet made it quite clear that she was the obvious person to captain the side and would also – she was firm about that too – keep wicket. 'Not much gets past me, you know', she'd said, putting her hands on her ample hips and bending her knees very slightly to demonstrate. Maisie said she and her sister could be the opening bats, Brenda surprised Ariel by claiming to be a 'nifty spin bowler' and Joy was keen to be one of the opening bowlers. Ariel and Alice Beck had both said they knew they couldn't bat or bowl anything like well enough to be key players, but had happily agreed to be on the team to make up the numbers. Arthur Foster had volunteered to take over the scoring and, just this once, tea would be brought in.

Two or three other names were mentioned as possibilities, but they were still one short. 'Which side you playing for then, Patrick?' Johnnie Beck had said, causing loud roars of laughter round the table. Patrick had simply smiled his glorious smile. The conversation had then changed direction, cake plates had needed to be replenished, and Ariel had put it all firmly out of her mind. Sort of.

But she couldn't help thinking about it on the drive home, so she'd said to Maisie, 'why did Johnnie ask Patrick which side he'd be playing for?'

'Because he thinks Patrick is gay, I suppose,' Maisie had responded.

'Is he?' The question was out before she could stop it.

'I don't know for sure but the general feeling is that he probably is. Janet is adamant about it; I'm surprised she hasn't said anything to you yet. But don't you know? You're better placed to know than any of us. After all, doesn't he come round the Parkers to babysit with you every week?'

'Yes, but it's only been friendly sort of stuff. Not boyfriend-girlfriend at all. Although Joy hinted ages ago that he'd said nice things about me. She seemed to think he would be interested in me in that way.'

Maisie had shrugged eloquently. 'That's Joy for you; can't see the wood for the trees. Or else she's so determined that he's not gay that she exaggerates anything that looks like what she'd call normal, I suppose. Bill doesn't think he's anything actually, do you, Bill?'

'What?'

'Patrick. You don't think he's gay or straight, do you?'

'Don't know and don't actually care, really. Mind you, Johnnie Beck's showing his ignorance: gay men don't particularly see themselves as females, as I understand it.' He'd shaken his head. 'Here you are, Ariel. See you next week.'

Nothing had changed, she told herself again. And again. Or had it? She couldn't be sure, just as, apparently, no one was really sure about Patrick. Janet Foster was convinced he was gay, and Joy was apparently convinced he was not, but for everyone else it seemed to be a question mark, just as it had apparently been for Pat. Why? What had led Pat to think that about him when she'd never even met him? And hadn't Pat asked her if she was turned on by him and hadn't she had to admit – to herself if not to Pat – that she was not? But did that mean he was gay? Maybe it meant more about her than about him. She shook her head and sat up in bed.

So okay, no sleep, so what to do instead? What would Pat

do? Could she phone her tomorrow and ask? Or should she ask Ellen's advice? She could do both, but that didn't solve the immediate problem of what to do now, instead of sleeping. There wasn't enough traffic for her to count cars, so she decided to see how many words she could make from the phrase 'nothing has changed'. Not, thing, thin, changing, hanging, hang, dang, sang, note, dote, shin, shit, shed, noting, hating, boring…oh no, there wasn't a b. But it was boring all the same, and not helping her to fall asleep. Maybe she should work on the whole phrase: 'nothing has changed except my perception of it'.

She pondered on that and thought, really, that was probably true of every situation you could think of. Because nothing ever changed unless you perceived its change. A bit like the tree falling in the forest, and only making a noise if someone was there? It could have been her offering for a quote that nobody could argue with. Would Mr Woods have given her an A for it? Perhaps he would have liked it better than the one she'd eventually offered, which had been, she had to admit, a bit of a cop-out. A or no A.

She missed his class. What else did he teach, she wondered. Whatever it was, she'd like to sign up for it in the autumn term, whether or not it would enhance her university prospects. Going to university wasn't all that attractive at the moment, not yet, at any rate – she wasn't anything like ready – but being in a Jack Woods class certainly was.

She settled into her pillows again and pondered on what sort of class Mr Woods could teach that she wouldn't sign up for. Well, car maintenance certainly, but then he probably wouldn't be teaching that. Or sugar sculpture, whatever that was. She began thinking of silly titles for silly classes….

●

She must have slept because when she looked at the clock it was quarter to ten. With a deep sigh she got out of bed, pulled on a jumper over her pyjamas and went downstairs, where she found

Howard, who was on nights this week, making himself breakfast.

'You look as if you haven't slept much. What's up?' Howard put a mug of coffee on the table in front of her.

'Thanks. I haven't. And I'm glad I'm not supposed to be anywhere this morning.' She sipped her coffee with pleasure. Howard made wonderful coffee and he took great pride in doing so. 'I suppose Ellen has already gone to work?'

'Actually she hasn't. She's having what she calls a mental health day, so if you want to take her up a coffee and some toast, I'm sure she'd be pleased.'

'Oh, okay. I will. Is she all right? She's not ill is she?'

'Nope, just temporarily fed up with the library I think. Drink your coffee and I'll make up a tray for the two of you.'

Ariel took the tray upstairs and knocked on the parents' bedroom door. She couldn't remember the last time she'd been in their room and felt slightly odd about it this morning. Ellen called 'come in' and smiled broadly when she saw Ariel with the tray. She put down the newspaper she'd been reading. 'Caught me bunking off! Here, sit down and tell me how things are for you. You look a bit rough this morning – what's on your mind?'

'You, at the moment – are you all right?'

'Absolutely. I've got a routine dentist's appointment this afternoon so I thought I just wouldn't go in at all today, rather than get stuck into something and then have to leave. So back to you.'

'The ladies at the cricket club all seem to think Patrick is gay.' Ariel couldn't think of a less abrupt way to start, so decided to plunge right in.

Ellen frowned slightly. 'Yes. I thought he probably was. And I suppose I've assumed you'd realised it too. But you hadn't? Were you thinking of him as boyfriend material?'

'That's the silly part – I wasn't, I didn't feel attracted to him in that way at all, but I think I sort of expected to sooner or later. So I keep telling myself that nothing has changed, he's a great friend and we seem to enjoy each other's company.'

'So it's not really a problem then? Or am I missing something?'

'Nooo, I don't think so. I don't know.' She thought for a minute. 'How does everybody else know that and I don't? I think that might be what's niggling me.'

Ellen smiled and shook her head. 'Give yourself a break! You're only sixteen and whilst some of your experiences have been far in advance of other teenagers', you've also missed out on an awful lot of so-called normal stuff.'

'Yes, you're probably right. In fact I know you are. And I think I probably knew that anyway, so why am I still fretting about this?'

'Do you feel a bit foolish that you are the only one not to know? That could be the issue, rather than the loss of Patrick as a potential boyfriend.'

'Hm, you may have something there. Are Janet and the tea ladies laughing at me behind my back? Probably not, actually. I don't think I've indicated to anyone that I might be interested in him in that way. Because in truth, I wasn't. And actually I've got what I want, haven't I? Patrick is a friend and I don't have to worry about whether or not he wants to kiss me.'

'You know what, a lot of my friends say the same thing about having gay mates. As you are wont to say, nothing has changed, so just enjoy Patrick's friendship. Yes?'

'Yes. I think I will. Thanks.' She drank her coffee and took the empty tray back downstairs feeling that Ellen had said the right things to let her do that.

And later in the week Pat said more or less the same thing. 'For crying-out-loud, most females I know would give one or more of their back teeth to have a solid friendship and not have to fend off wandering hands all the time. And when you're ready for a bit of that, I'll fix you up with another mate of Glyn's if you like.'

'Thanks. But not yet. And not an Ivor-clone, please.'

TWENTY-SEVEN

Saturday

Crikey, the last thing I wrote (and heavily crossed out) in here was Ariel Cavendish! Which reminds me that I'm ready to ask the parents to start calling me Ariel – if they will. I'm pretty sure Ellen will, and probably Howard will too, once Ellen tells him to. This is step one to making the final decision about my name. I've decided to take it one step at a time rather than try to work out now how I'm going to feel in six months about the rest of my name. That's quite a relief! As is realising that it's really only a choice between Dee and Pike; I don't need to confuse the issue with other possibilities.

I'm really looking forward to seeing Patrick this evening and NOT having to worry about will he/won't he. I wonder if he'll notice any difference in me.

Pat is going away for ten days. Glyn is taking her to Italy to celebrate his birthday. 'Very fond of Italy, is my Glyn,' she said, then quoted Verdi (I think): 'You may have the universe if I may have Italy'. I was impressed and told her so. She was pleased, and said she'd looked for a quote to put on Glyn's birthday card and this is what she came up with. She couldn't remember who said it though! What a lovely and loving thing to do for him. I wonder what sort of quote I could put on a birthday card for Patrick when he turns twenty-three later this month. I'm assuming that wouldn't be inappropriate – to give him a birthday card. I'll ask Ellen what she thinks. About the card, not about the quote. I'll probably ask Pat, too, although I'm feeling better able to make my own decisions because she and I don't always see eye-to-eye about these things. I'm very aware that I've been sort of watching her to see how to do things, what to feel, how to react – in much the same way as I did with Will. Perhaps it's a sign of growing up that I need to do this less and less. And that when I have a different opinion from hers, it's mostly okay.

Hurray for me.

I don't particularly FEEL very grown up though...

•

Somewhat to Ariel's surprise, Patrick opened the door to her when she arrived at the Parkers.

'Goodness, am I glad to see you! I've only been alone with them for twenty-five minutes and I'm knackered already. I don't know how you – and Joy – do it.'

He didn't look particularly worn out, Ariel thought, as she smiled back at him. 'I'll put the kettle on and get the tea going. Wash your hands for tea, boys,' she called as she went through to the kitchen, followed by Patrick. 'So Joy just abandoned you, then?'

'Sort of, though in a way it was planned. She's gone to see Eric before she meets up with Clive. He – Eric – asked me to drop in here early, so when he rang to ask her to meet him, she'd be able to leave straight away. He wants to tell her he got engaged on Wednesday.'

'What? Crikey!' Ariel sat down at the kitchen table, unable to formulate the next logical sentence. 'I thought... I mean, they...'

'Yes, I know.' Patrick sat down opposite her. 'Let me just say quickly that it's going to be all right. She'll be all right about it, she already knows about the woman, although being Joy she's been reluctant to see it for what it really is. I'll tell you all about it when the boys are in bed.'

'Of course.' She took a deep breath and told herself she had to get through the next hour and a half or so as normally as possible. She had to put all thoughts of Joy, Eric, Clive, Patrick, and anything else related to them, right out of her head. Over the years she'd had plenty of practice at that. 'Okay, troops, cheese on toast coming right up for all those sitting at the table with clean hands.'

Somehow she managed. Looking back on the evening, she didn't think the boys would have detected anything was amiss. Patrick helped enormously by telling them silly jokes and asking them silly riddles, whilst she made toast, melted cheese, drew ketchup faces on it and poured cups of milk. ('We aren't really allowed ketchup,' Graham had whispered. 'Well it won't matter just this once,' she'd responded conspiratorially, thinking that would probably take their mind off just about anything.) She couldn't eat, even the tea was hard to swallow, but somehow she managed and by half past seven both boys were fed, bathed, storied and asleep. She went downstairs.

Patrick had made her a fresh mug of tea and opened a bottle of cider for himself. 'Shall I just launch in, or do you want to ask questions?'

'I can't make sense of it,' she kept shaking her head. 'I thought they were, you know, "an item". I think some of the women at the cricket club thought they were, too. I keep thinking of them on the London trip...'

'Yes, that wasn't good. I felt quite ashamed of all of us that you'd had to witness that behaviour. I read them both the riot act about it – which may have been what nudged Eric to get on with it and actually get engaged. He's been seeing this woman, Olga, for over two years.'

'Oh my god! Didn't Joy know?'

'She did. But she refused to take it seriously. And Eric didn't help there – coming to London for example, how could she believe he and Olga were a genuine couple? She's managed to persuade herself that because he, Eric, couldn't actually have her, he needed somewhere to release his passion and I suppose she saw Olga as a safe place for him to do that.'

'What will she do now?' Ariel thought she could feel Joy's pain, likening it to her own pain of losing Will. Only worse in a way; Joy would have to see Eric with another woman. She went cold at the thought of seeing Will with another 'daughter'.

'Well one of the reasons he wanted to do it now, this evening I mean, is so she can turn to Clive for comfort.'

'Clive knows?' Ariel was staggered. 'And he didn't stop it

happening?'

'Oh yes, he's known all along. His position is that he loves Joy so much that whatever makes her happy makes him happy.'

'Even to the point of her being unfaithful? I don't think I could manage that.'

'I don't think many men – or women – could, but that's the line he's taken and he's determined to stick with it. I suppose that's how he lives with the situation. But for the record, I don't think they've actually consummated this relationship. Although it could easily be argued that you don't have to have sex to be unfaithful.' Patrick sighed. 'It's a mess, and I'm sorry you are caught up in it. I really am.'

'Well it's not your fault. But this woman – Olga? – she never comes to cricket matches.'

'No, evidently it's not her scene. I worry, actually, that she may put an end to his cricket career sooner or later. Which of course will give Joy more fuel for her fast-burgeoning fantasy that Eric is henpecked by Olga, alas, when actually he's head over heels in love with the woman. And she with him, as far as I can see.'

'Doesn't Joy know that?'

'She's brilliant, my sister, at not seeing what's right in front of her, and not taking in what she doesn't want to see. She's the same with me – absolutely and resolutely refuses to acknowledge that I'm gay. Hence her rather obvious pushing me in your direction and you in mine. And I don't feel very clean about that either, I need to tell you. It doesn't sit well with me that she pretends to think that I have what she calls "a thing" for you. In truth I come round here when you're babysitting because I like being with you, I enjoy your company and I think you enjoy mine. And I especially like the fact that you aren't throwing yourself at me and wanting something other than friendship. A good friendship is priceless and I feel very lucky, honoured even, that you and I might be forming a lifelong connection as good, solid friends.'

'I feel the same.' Ariel was aware there wasn't even a

nanosecond pause between the end of his small speech and her firm reply, yet the speed of her thoughts – should she admit she hadn't known that he was gay or should she pretend she'd known all along – and the rapid decision to opt for the latter, made her so dizzy that she had to close her eyes for a moment. She would be glad when this evening was over so she could snuggle into her own bed and let her thoughts spin and swirl until they fell into some sort of pattern that she could make sense of. 'I feel very lucky to have met you.' She smiled at him. 'I'm beginning to think of you as sort of an older brother.' She hadn't expected to say that, but as soon as she did, she knew it was true. She felt an almost physical sensation in her brain as various thoughts and concerns seemed to settle into their rightful places.

•

'I have something to ask you.' Ariel had slept better than she'd expected after Patrick's revelation and had decided, on waking, she would tackle the name question with the parents that very morning. Then she would take herself off to the cricket and think about that. She tried not to think about Patrick's declaration, or about Joy – who had seemed her usual cheerful self when she and Clive returned from their evening out. Hopefully she'd be no different this afternoon. Crikey, she'd have a lot to tell Pat when her friend returned from Italy.

'Oh yes?' Howard looked expectantly at her and then at Ellen who smiled briefly, then squashed it and assumed an inquiring look.

'I wonder how you'd feel about calling me Ariel instead of Jessica. Actually, no, I want you to call me Ariel. Though I do want to know how you feel about it, too.' Somehow that hadn't come out quite as she'd rehearsed, but the parents didn't look too horrified. Ellen was nodding and smiling broadly again. Howard looked... what? She couldn't tell what his reaction was.

He spoke first. 'Well I can't say it's actually taken us by surprise.'

'In fact, we've talked about it,' Ellen interjected. 'But go on,

Howard.'

'She's right, we have, and I think we've both felt it was inevitable after you started college and got in with the Parkers and go by Ariel with them. I can't honestly say I have any strong feelings about Jessica as a name, but equally, I can't say I'm wildly enthusiastic about Ariel as a name either.'

'It's just because you're not used to it, love. I've been trying to think of her as Ariel for a few weeks now, so I'm more used to it. I quite like it, too,' slightly defiantly. 'I think you'd get used to it, too, Howard, if you'd give it a go. Will you?' Ellen reached across the breakfast table and took her husband's hand, looking anxiously at his face.

'Of course I will. I'll do my best, anyway. I'm sure I'll forget sometimes, so bear with me. I'm an old man you know.'

'You are not! Paul's an old man, you have decades to go before you get there.' Ariel was so relieved at how easy this had turned out to be that she allowed her indignation to flow. 'But thank you, thank you both so much. It's turning out to be terribly important to me.'

'We never thought it wasn't,' Howard smiled. 'So go for it and hopefully you won't feel the need to change your last name then. If you're still thinking about it, that is.'

Ariel was ready for this one. 'I'm not thinking about it at the moment, but that doesn't mean it's permanently off the cards. I've decided to go one step at a time and for the moment becoming Ariel officially is all I want to manage. I think I'll send for the deed poll forms then, if you're sure you're okay about it?'

She could see Howard gulping slightly. Perhaps he hadn't realised she planned to make it official so quickly. She also saw Ellen increase the pressure on his hand.

'Go for it, kid,' Howard said heartily. 'I mean, Ariel. And then maybe one day you could return the favour by calling me Dad.'

She decided to pretend she hadn't heard that as she got up

and went round the table. She dropped a kiss on the top of his bristly head, realising as she did so, that she'd never so much as even hugged him before. 'Crikey,' she thought, 'all sorts of changes going on here. But I think I'm liking them!'

•

Cricket didn't look too likely that afternoon. Ariel stood at the end of their road in the pouring rain waiting for the Parker's minivan, and wondered whether it was even worth their going to the Ponteland ground. She also wondered how they would all pass the time, cloistered in the pavilion, and whether all would be normal between Eric and Joy. And between Joy and Clive. She supposed she'd be left to look after the boys if she wasn't going to be occupied with scoring, and she wondered how on earth she could entertain them under these circumstances.

She looked at her watch. They were late, they ought to have been here fifteen minutes ago. Maybe the match had been called off on account of the rain, but surely they would have phoned to tell her. Perhaps they had phoned after she left; should she go back home to check? But then, what if they came and she wasn't there? She'd give them another fifteen minutes, she reasoned, and then decide what to do next.

She wasn't unhappy standing there, dry under her umbrella; she had lots to think about. The relief at having Patrick's gay status out in the open was growing and growing, and she kept re-feeling her contentment at his declaration of his feelings of friendship. There was also a huge relief at how easily her name-change request had gone over. Ellen had been easy enough to get along with from the start, but had Howard always been this palpably contented with life? Hadn't he been a bit more prickly when she'd first moved to live with them? Perhaps it was Ellen's influence. She seemed to be able to have a soothing effect on almost any difficult issue. She couldn't think about his request to call him Dad yet. But she would, eventually. Think about it, that is.

Thirty-five minutes late now. They must not be coming, they must have left a message. She turned to walk back up the road and saw Howard coming towards her. 'Match is cancelled,' he shouted as he drew closer, 'come home and get dry.'

They walked back up the road together. 'Ellen's a bit under the weather this afternoon,' he said as they went through the gate. 'She didn't want you to worry, so she didn't say anything this morning, but she's gone to bed for the afternoon thinking you'd be out for the rest of the day.'

'Oh no! What's wrong?' Ariel felt her contentment vanish as the anxiety about Ellen poured in to take its place.

'She'll tell you, I expect. Women's problems.'

'Oh, the curse.' Relief returned, along with a sense of pride at knowing the right word to use with Howard. 'Thanks, Pat,' she thought, and was suddenly nearly overwhelmed with a realisation of how much she was missing her friend. She'd use the unexpectedly free afternoon to write to her. She didn't know her address in Italy, of course, but she could have the letter done and ready for Pat's return. She'd also make tea for Howard and Ellen, she decided. It had been ages since she'd made a cake; that would be a good rainy day activity. She'd been keeping an envelope with recipes to try; she'd see if they had the ingredients for something from her stack.

TWENTY-EIGHT

Saturday

A boring week. And how could it be otherwise after last weekend? Enough amazing things on Saturday and Sunday to keep any intensity-addict satisfied. I'd been afraid Sunday would deteriorate into a massive anti-climax when the cricket was cancelled. But no, the excitement continued when Ellen told me, after raving over my chocolate orange sponge cake, that she is pregnant! No wonder she and Howard look so smugly satisfied with life. The baby is due in February and all is going well, except that she is very tired and gets periods of being sick. Hence the retreat to bed on Sunday afternoon and, I suspect, the Monday morning in bed a couple of weeks ago. She says it's all normal and there is nothing to worry about, but of course I do. And so does Howard. As well he should.

Bless her, she was worried I might not be pleased! Silly woman! She doesn't see me going all gooey over Graham and Nigel. I'm so thrilled I've hardly been able to concentrate on anything else. She says she's not particularly maternal so will be more than happy to let me do as much as I want to with the baby. At the same time, she insisted there will be no obligation to do anything, if I prefer it that way. I can't imagine that, frankly.

I want to learn to knit so I can make some baby jumpers for my new sibling. Thank heavens college is ending next week and that there isn't an exam to study for. It's a take-home paper and I've been working on it for a fortnight now so feel it will be at least adequate. It's been hard to concentrate on it, and it proved impossible to settle down and write to Pat as I'd planned to before I got the baby news.

What will they call it? Howard says they haven't got that far yet, but I'll bet Ellen has some ideas. I shall be careful to endorse her preferences and not make a fuss if they choose something I don't like. Like Chardonnay or Wilbert! They won't, I'm sure. I think.

Pat will be home tomorrow. I'll be so happy to see her – I'm going round after lunch on Monday – and have SO much to tell her. I hope she had a great time.

•

'Do you know who Brian Taft is?'

Ariel shook her head. 'No?'

'He's part of your birthday present. Well, sort of. And sorry it's taken so long.'

'Well I hope he's not like Ivor.' Ariel smiled, but Pat wasn't smiling back.

'No, he's not like Ivor. In many ways he's a lot worse than Ivor, though I know you haven't thought so. You might though, when I've finished.'

'Pat, what are you talking about? Please stop speaking in riddles. Who is Brian Taft and how is he part of my birthday present please?'

Pat handed her a photocopied picture that had obviously been printed in a newspaper. 'This is Brian Taft. Recognise him? You should – you've slept with him, as well as kissed him pretty juicily.'

Ariel thought she was going to faint. The photograph was clearly Will, albeit taken several years before she knew him. His hair was shorter, he was wearing glasses and his face was thinner, but it was still him. She propped herself against Pat's kitchen table and tried to speak, but when she opened her mouth all that came out was a sort of strangled gurgle. She held her breath.

Pat put her arms around her and pulled out a chair, pushing her onto it. 'Here, sit down for god's sake. And breathe! Ariel! Breathe!' She pulled another chair alongside and sat as close to Ariel as she could without actually sitting right on her.

Ariel gulped a huge intake of air, blew it out and then took another. 'Oh jesus, don't hyperventilate now,' Pat panicked. 'Sit still, breathe normally, and let me tell you what I've found out. You may hate me and I know you don't want to hear it, but in the end you have to and you'll be all the better for it. Okay?'

Ariel nodded. She had to know. She couldn't stop this happening now. 'Okay,' she whispered, clinging hard to the edge of the table, and looked at the photograph. 'Where did this come from? How did you get this? How did you find it?'

'It wasn't hard. I've warned you before that I'm not the little thickhead some people like to think I am. I've listened to you all these months and got a good idea of dates, places and things, so a little diligent research of newspapers and police files in the public domain, and voila! It all falls into place.'

'What all falls into place? What do you mean?' Ariel found her voice.

'Will Dee, who is actually Brian Taft, was a serial abductor, who not so incidentally murdered your two predecessors: the two fake Ariel Durants before you, who evidently didn't come up to scratch for this lovely man. So he offed 'em, and dumped their bodies into the sea off the north of Scotland. That's how lovely your Will Dee was. And that's why the police were so interested in him even after he was killed. And that's whose clothes were in those boxes marked A-I and A-II. Clothes of murdered girls, Ariel, clothes that you wore!' The increasing shrillness of Pat's voice was like fingernails on the chalkboard to Ariel.

'How do you know? He wasn't interviewed or anything, he couldn't have told anyone because he was dead. This is all conjecture.' Ariel felt her strength returning. She was getting ready to fight.

'No, not conjecture at all. That's the sweet part – he kept a journal, didn't he? Classic psychopath behaviour that is, apparently. It was all in there, according to the reports. He may have been smashed to smithereens, but his hard drive survived just fine, thank you, and the police had a field day reading his sickening ramblings about a girl he nicked from a travellers' camp in Somerset and another he picked up in France. And – hold my hand hard – there were times when he planned to kill you too.'

'That's not true. He didn't, he loved me. I don't want to hear this, so stop! Stop now!' Ariel pulled away from Pat and put her hands over her ears.

'Well you've heard it now. And you do want to know. You must. You've got to see the truth so you can move on with your life. Ariel – take your hands off your ears and LISTEN to me.'

Ariel took her hands away from her ears but only so she could cover her face. She began sobbing. She was shaking so hard the table actually rattled. Pat said nothing but held onto Ariel's upper arm, stroking it soothingly and making little crooning noises.

'I'm sorry you're upset about it, Ariel, but I can't feel any remorse for doing it.' Pat finally broke the awkward silence. 'I wanted to know who he was and what he thought he was doing with you. I also wanted to free you from him; he's been living rent-free in your head all this time and that isn't healthy.'

Ariel thought that if a person knew she was about to go completely berserk, this would be what it felt like. She clung desperately to the table, at the same time aware that she couldn't really feel it. It wasn't her table and it didn't feel right. Something was happening to her arm, too, but she couldn't work out what it was or what to do about it. She hoped it wouldn't interfere with her ability to knit for Ellen and Howard's baby. Oh that's right, she was going to walk over to the shopping centre when she left here to buy some wool and a pattern so she could start right away. Had she told Pat about the baby yet? She couldn't remember. There was something else she needed to talk to Pat about, too. What was that? And for that matter, what was the other part of her birthday present?

Her arm still felt odd, but the sensation of something actually happening to it seemed to have stopped. There was a mug of tea in front of her now, too. Was that for her to drink? How had it got there?

'Ariel? Ariel, come on hen-chick, drink your tea and talk to me. What's going on?'

The voice was familiar. Oh, yes, it was Pat. She'd probably made the tea. Good, now they could have a chat about the baby and the other thing that she couldn't, for the moment, remember. She looked up and smiled at her friend. 'I've got something really exciting to tell you. Two things, actually, but I seem to have forgotten one of them.'

•

They walked over to the shopping centre and found the wool shop. Ariel was aware that Pat kept looking at her, worriedly, and it began to irritate her. 'I'm all right, stop looking at me all the time.'

'Okay, if you say so, though you don't seem all right to me. But I'll try to keep my concerns to myself for a bit. We'll get the baby wool stuff and then we'll huddle in the coffee shop for a bit and talk some more. Yes?'

'We'll see. At the moment I only want to talk about the baby, and a little bit about Patrick. I think I need to have some time to think about the other stuff – and get over my fury at you, my friend, at what you've done. But I don't want to go into that now. I need to not think about it actually.' Ariel tried to sound calm and firm.

'Fair enough,' Pat sighed. 'I can be patient. But not for too long, it's not in my nature.'

Ariel made her selection from the massive racks of various colours and textures. The shop assistant showed her appropriate knitting patterns and made sure she had the right sized needles, and they were done.

'What did you want to say about Patrick, then?' Pat steered Ariel across the car park and into Starbucks where they found a vacant comfy sofa in a quiet corner.

'Only that he is gay. He brought it up in the most matter-of-fact way that I felt absolutely unable to express anything other than a sort of "oh yes, I knew that and I'm perfectly okay about it" kind of attitude. I didn't actually have to say anything, he just dropped it into the conversation we were having about his sister and Eric. Oh, yes, that's over, too. Eric has just popped the question to his long-time girlfriend!'

'Bloody hell! "May you live in interesting times" as the Chinese say – only they mean it as a curse. You certainly do! Blimey Ariel, this is MUCH more interesting than Ellen and Howard's forthcoming sprog. Spill!'

Ariel related the events of the past couple of weeks with as much detail as she could remember, knowing, with pleasure, that Pat was interested and enthralled. She glossed over her own distress at what she'd heard at the cricket match; in fact, she was beginning to remember that she had always been quite sanguine about it, thus considerably playing down the anguish she'd felt before her conversation with Ellen. 'In a way I'm relieved. It's so nice to have a sort of older brother kind of friend and not worry about whether it's going to turn into something else all the time.'

'Well, you said all along you didn't know if you really fancied him. So I think you probably did know, in your heart of hearts, that he isn't available, so to speak. And, not to change the subject entirely – or bring up a sore point – but do you think the kind of friendship you are envisioning with him would be a sort of replacement for the kind of thing you had – or wanted to have – with Will? Only with Patrick it would be real; he probably isn't grooming you for the starring role in his bizarre drama.'

Ariel's pleasure in the moment vanished. 'Oh damn it, Pat, why did you bring that up again? I told you I need to think in my own time about it. I don't want to think about it now – it makes me too angry with YOU. I'm trying to pretend that you are still my best friend when really I think I never want to see you again.' She stopped, afraid of what she might say that could never be repaired. 'Sorry. I don't think I really meant that.'

'You probably do, but I'm hoping you'll get over it because if you don't then the psychology course is going to be a bit awkward.'

'What psychology course? What are you talking about?'

Ariel stopped feeling she was about to cry and stared at Pat.

'That's the other part of your birthday present, except that I have to be honest and say that I'm not really only doing it for you. To my utter amazement, I find I've signed up for Psychology 101 for the whole bloody year and if you don't sign up too I'm going to be well pissed off with you.'

'I thought you said you'd never...why psychology?' Ariel could hardly believe she'd heard Pat correctly. Her thoughts galloped on...they'd be in college together again...for a whole year...they'd be learning about psychology - why people did the things they did...and she'd be doing it with Pat! They'd be able to have their after-class hot chocolate drinks and chats in the cafeteria again. 'But I haven't signed up for anything yet,' reality crept back in, 'what if they're full?'

'They aren't. I've checked and double-checked, and I've told the registrar that you'll be signing up. So what say we jump on the bus now and get that done and dusted? If we're still friends, of course...'

'Oh Pat! You are the most wonderful and the most contrary person I've ever met. And I hate you at the moment, too.'

'I know, I can live with that for a bit. Come on, swig up and let's get down the college before they all go home for the night.'

'I'll have to have the parents' signature – will they let me sign up and get the form back to them when Howard or Ellen has signed it?'

'Of course they will. They want people to sign up. And you have a record there, so there won't be any problem. Come ON!'

They hurried out to the bus stop and quickly caught the appropriate bus. 'See, it was meant to be,' Pat said, 'the very first bus to come along was the right one.'

'Paul wants me to take more than one thing; I'll have to ask him on Monday what else I should sign up for. He thinks I should be more or less full time this year.'

'That's settled then, you do that. Stop worrying! And don't leave your blasted knitting gubbins on the bus, either.'

Signing up was as simple as Pat had suggested and was

accomplished, Howard's signature pending, in less than ten minutes. 'Cafeteria?' Pat looked her hopefully. 'For old times' sake?'

'Okay. Then you can tell me why you've changed your mind about taking another college course please.'

'Simples. I want to understand your peculiar mind. I want to know how you can shut things off and pretend they aren't happening and I want to learn why people like you latch onto dead people like the Durants, and C S Lewis, not to mention Will, why you seem to need something like that to keep you going. You know what? And this might shock you even more than it shocks me, but for the first time in my life I'm interested in somebody other than me! I think I'm going to be a psychologist before I'm done. I've discovered I like learning what makes people tick. I'll have to take the odd A-level to really go all the way with it, but I'll jump off that bridge when I come to it. Mea

TWENTY-NINE

Saturday

I wonder if other people's journals are as full of turmoil as mine. The current turn of events seems bigger than anything that's gone before – or am I making too big a meal out of it? Even so, it doesn't seem to be tearing me apart as I thought it would have. Pat says she's in awe of how I distance myself from feelings when I have to; she keeps saying that's one of the reasons she wants to study psychology: she wants to understand me. Yeah, me too! (Yet C S Lewis was the same; apparently because of his early experiences he learned how to put things he didn't want to feel behind a sort of 'firewall' in his mind. I like it that he and I have that in common.)

I'm thrilled about her doing the course with me. I'd half thought about psychology being one of the three things I'd take, but hadn't really firmed anything up. Paul is pushing me towards English literature (only not with the Barrett Dragon; even he admits she's a bit much, though actually I think I could possibly manage her again now) and says he'd be fine about another philosophy course (hopefully with Mr Woods) to round out the programme. He'll continue to mentor my progress, he says, and to be honest I quite like the idea that there is someone to answer to. (Other than Pat, of course, who will always keep me on my toes, but perhaps not always in a good-for-me-ultimately direction.) I've got all the forms from the college and Howard (Dad!!) is happy to sign whatever I ask him to. He's so cloud-niney about the baby I think he'd buy me a car if I asked him. Hmm... I wonder... No, not yet. And not yet on the calling him 'Dad' front, either. But perhaps it will come.

So, college – and plans for the coming year – all sorted. Patrick ditto, as long as I go on babysitting for the Parkers, I assume. Although now that we are 'officially friends' I suppose it doesn't have to be only there. And anyway, still a few more cricket Sundays before that's all finished for the season. Even Joy and Eric seem sorted. Unless Joy is in what Pat would say is total denial. She (Joy) seems fine about it all. Still being all touchy-feely with Eric at cricket teatimes and, as far as I can tell, not unhappy about the situation at all. If Pat wants to see somebody really 'dissociate' (she's already into psychological jargon, which can be intensely irritating) she should observe Joy Parker.

Actually, not only is she (Pat, not Joy!) spouting psychobabble every chance she gets, she's already read three books on beginning psychology and told me yesterday that she understands my anger at her as a displacement for the anger I'm really feeling at Will but can't yet allow it in. I've always thought she was very wise so I'm not dismissing her diagnosis entirely, annoying though she is with it all. Perhaps I should read the same books so I can match her babble for babble. I might actually learn something helpful, too.

And how am I feeling about Pat now? I keep telling myself I hate her because of what she did, but then I look back at what I've just written! I'm over the moon at the prospect of going to college with her for a whole year! How can that be? (And here's where I can hear Mr Woods warning me off black and white thinking! It's perhaps okay to feel two apparently conflicting feelings at the same time!)

In any case, I don't do hate. And I could never be indifferent to Pat.

I'm actually feeling quite numb about Will (so she could well be right about my displaced anger). I think I might also be feeling a bit relieved to finally know what he's done. I don't believe he didn't care for me, though. And I don't think I was just one in a string of possible 'Ariels'. I may have been at the start, but I'm pretty sure he truly loved me (in his own peculiar way perhaps) because of who and how I was. Perhaps I need to believe that? But actually, does it matter? The truth is that I felt truly loved for probably the first time in my life, and learned so much from Will that I can never fully regret what happened in those two years.

I've done a lot of thinking about it since Pat's horrific revelation. She said he'd planned to murder me (according to his journal). But he didn't murder me. Far from it; he gave me a very nice life really. It was certainly a better life than I'd ever have had with that vile and abusive Jock and my pathetic passive mother. And in the end I've got what I'd initially wanted: I'm living with my real dad who grows on me steadily and his lovely Ellen whom I adore. I'll never have to see Jock (or Will!) again. I think I could probably manage to forget it all if I worked at it, but oddly I don't think I want to. I think I can take the best of the experience and I've survived the worst.

AND: I've made the final decision about my name. I'm keeping Ariel because that's who I've become, but there is no way in the world I'm taking the Dee name now. (In any case, Dee wasn't even Will's real name, and I certainly wouldn't want Taft as my last name!). No, I'm staying Pike. With some pride, I have to say. In a few months I'll have a baby sister with the same last name, and that's hugely important to me now.

•••

About the Author

Margaret Pitz has been writing stories in her head for as long as she can remember. She has now had three novels published.

Also by the Author

Finding Dad (2013)

10-year-old Jessie Pike sets off to find her father, leaving an uncaring mother and abusive stepfather. She is picked up by Will, a man who will stop at nothing to fulfil a specific fantasy. Will's dream requires Jessie to become someone else but to what extent is it possible to brainwash a child? And could Jessie's search for a father coincide with Will's fantasy? This novel raises fundamental questions about the adult-child relationship, which will linger in your mind long after you've read the final page.

Alice in Madland (2015)

It's 1958 and 17-year-old Alice Chorley's career aspirations are in tatters. She takes a mindless office job where she is drawn into – and colludes with – the mad fantasy world of senior secretary Pearl Taylor. Their 'Game' is played out in counterpoint to Alice's more normal (though unsatisfactory) relationship with her boyfriend, Jack. The fantasies escalate and the tension mounts, leading to an explosive confrontation, a startling revelation and, ultimately, a different life for Alice.

Praise for *After Dad*

*"Powerful, but gently appointed, a book for someone looking for a really good read...." (*Reviews: Amazon.co.uk)